PAPABILE

The Man Who
Would Be Pope

— A NOVEL —

Michael J. Farrell

A Crossroad Book
The Crossroad Publishing Company
New York

The Crossroad Publishing Company
370 Lexington Avenue, New York, NY 10017

Printed in the United States of America

Library of Congress Cataloging-in-Publication Data
Farrell, Michael J.
    Papabile : the man who would be pope : a novel / Michael J.
Farrell.
        p.   cm.
    ISBN 0-8245-1730-X (pbk.)
    I. Title.
PS3556.A7714P36   1998
813'.54–dc21   97-40715

1   2   3   4   5   6   7   8   9   10   02   01   00   99   98

For Marilyn

Chapter One

Only a beginning had been made. There would be many a broken heart, many a stab of pain, many a cry of betrayal before people realized that the old ways were gone and that they themselves were flame of the new fire, and then somewhere down the long road the charred world might become cities of gold and countryside of green and laughing people waving.

Hugo felt this exhilaration every morning as he responded ardently to the shrill shouts of the drillmaster. He was twenty, tall, country-fresh, his coarse hair unruly, his big chest gleaming with sweat. He showed a fierce determination, his eyes fixed ahead, his mouth slightly open, out-performing everyone.

Black smoke emerged from a blackened chimney against a blue sky. The burnt-out house sat brooding, chunks of masonry blown away to leave gaping wounds. Swastikas and other Nazi relics were daubed on the remaining walls. A fire of logs in the old fireplace was sending up the sullen black smoke, a message to the countryside that there was still life up here. This building was one of a dozen, all dilapidated now, in a village nestled amid majestic mountains.

At the end of the village several hundred young men were learning to drill. The drillmaster strutted, officious as hell. The recruits looked eager but inept, most carrying mock wooden guns. The tattoo of their marching feet accentuated the stillness of the morning. A thick fog floated between the mountains. It made the rising sun look pale and silver like a moon. Blackened trees lifted their arms out of the grayness where war had stripped the green fields naked. The countryside was quiet and expecting, waiting patiently for the peasants who once rose stoically and sometimes even joyfully to wrestle with the earth and life, but now no longer saw any reason, crushed, the camps and the carnage etched on their faces and common consciousness, not yet ready to straighten their bent backs for one more surge of hope.

It was 1945 and Eastern Europe was rising from the ashes one more time.

The political dust had not yet settled. Many individuals and parties wanted to rule the country, either to rape or to redeem it. While the old guard, those with the wealth or breeding to rule the roost in the past, still held precarious sway, the Party already had real control, more substantial every day, backed by some and opposed by many. Above all, the Party had the Russian army (that was where power lay) scattered in every village, a constant threat, waiting for Hugo and his comrades to be ready, and then it would go home leaving this new generation powerful and significant, men of destiny.

As they stood to attention, Hugo heard a car come up the bleak mountain road. Others heard it too and turned their heads, but Hugo, rigid, would not turn. The drillmaster yelled in anger. Then the car was in Hugo's line of vision, three men emerging, approaching. It was hard to keep concentration — strangers were rare in the mountains.

The three stopped at a distance, casually observing.

"Ovath!" one of them eventually shouted. Moment of panic. Strangers were known to come and take people away, vague low talk among neighbors of terrible things done, fears and suspicions. Hugo walked between the rows of young men to where the three strangers waited.

"Is your name Hugo Ovath?"

"Yes." He wiped sweat from his forehead with the back of his hand. He was breathing heavily, his eyes animal-looking and questioning. He was so healthy and his big square face was so well made that the three were impressed.

"Come with us, then." The man who spoke was scarcely thirty, light and lean, his hair thinning already, sly looking like a fox, but hearty and feisty when not being sinister, a chameleon who revealed these qualities only gradually and as the occasion demanded.

"They're so damned young," the second man, whose name was Ivoski, said as they returned to the car. Ivoski was a big, surly, stupid man, a junior official of the enforcer breed.

Hugo waited for the others to go ahead of him, but the third man insisted with a grunt on bringing up the rear. A rotund, middle-aged bundle, he was known as the man from Moscow.

"Young but willing," the leader amended. "Hey — the old ones are bitter because of, you know, what happened. They hate Communism.

But look at those lads, eager for a cause. They listen to the song the future sings, intoxicated by the promise of a golden age."

"Please," protested Ivoski, "it's too early in the day for philosophy."

"It's not philosophy; it's poetry."

The man from Moscow said nothing, padding behind, small and round. The fog was lifting and the sun stronger, throwing morning shadows. Nearby, a thin cow sucked the spare dewy grass.

Ivoski drove. The man from Moscow grunted and gestured, and Hugo slipped into the back seat beside him. There was an acrid smell of gasoline. Hugo had never been in a car before, but his anxiety waned at the wonder of the speed, the ribbon of road ahead of them quickly eaten up.

The leader leaned back to observe Hugo. He was in a feisty but ingratiating mood.

"The good news is, Hugo — the Party is very pleased with your, you know, enthusiasm and initiative. Very pleased. And I hear you're an actor?"

"Only a little, sir. At university." It was amazing to Hugo, a nobody from the mountains, that this obviously important man should know his name. He had spent last year at the university, a gift from the new regime; his parents could never afford it. It was a reward for his enthusiasm. As the local Party bosses told it, only the young had the vision to see that Communism held the one real hope, would make rich and poor equal, the people fighting and working together for prosperity and dignity. It hurt like a physical pain to go against his parents, but the pain was made bearable by the hope that they would see in time the truth to which he was committed.

"And what part did you play?"

"Trigorin, sir. That was in *The Sea Gull*. By Chekhov, sir. And then I played..."

"Splendid! By God, boy, you're a find, a rare find, huh?" He gave Hugo a long, contemplative look, enough to make the raw youth feel exposed and uncomfortable. "You know who I am, boy?" he asked eventually.

"No, sir."

"Cut out that 'sir,' boy." Then after a further long silence, "I'm Zoltan Fust."

"Yes, sir."

"You're a howl, boy. Say it. Go on, be a daredevil and say it."

"Zoltan Fust."

"Splendid. On second thought, you could call me sir for now." He made a gesture toward his two companions. "These two here — do you know them? Of course not. They are — oh, never mind. You're so damned young, Hugo — by God, I wish I were that young and — well, here we are."

Big doors opened for the car. The word for police was inelegantly written in white paint on the wall, but it was clear that the building had once been a monastery. There were long cloistered walks on either side of the courtyard where the car had stopped, little diamond-paned windows with ivy encroaching, and a chunky bell tower ahead with an arched doorway beneath it.

To the side, a score of soldiers were loosely bunched, smoking and talking quietly or occasionally jostling one another good-naturedly. But there were guns in their hands. It was a picture of contradiction. White pigeons sat lazy on high ledges. Stained glass windows squinted toward the courtyard that Hugo supposed was once filled with song and prayer. And upstairs were smaller windows looking out from the cells where monks once wrestled with God and devils and themselves. Hugo wondered where they were now, dead or alive.

An officer came forward and saluted Fust, a gesture Fust ignored.

"How long?" asked Fust.

"Any minute now."

As Fust and the officer departed into the barracks, Ivoski sidled forward.

"I hope you're not squeamish." He spoke from the side of his mouth.

"Why?" Hugo asked.

"Are you?" Ivoski now asked fiercely, showing his dirty teeth.

"No."

Fust returned. The day was getting hot. Shouts and commotion could be heard from inside.

A carved, wooden door was thrown open, and two soldiers dragged out a young man who was shouting and resisting. He was about twenty-two, with a black growth of beard and wild eyes full of defiance.

"I'll see you all in hell, God damn you; I'll see you in hell," he repeated as he was dragged to the wall. An officer stepped forward. He tied a black band over the young man's eyes. The young man bit him, then laughed wildly, telling the officer he'd see him in hell. The officer, infuriated, struck the young man repeatedly in the face and stomach, then pulled off the black band. Whatever was going to happen, the young man would see it coming in advance.

"He's a subversive," Ivoski said at Hugo's side. Hugo wondered whether Ivoski was really a cruel man or was covering up his own squeamishness. "There are still many fanatics left, and there is only one thing to do with them."

The officer barked orders, and the soldiers came to attention, including six who formed a firing squad.

"Come up closer," Fust said suddenly, "for a better look."

"I can see from here." Hugo had lived through the war and seen violence and killing, but never anything personal and planned like this.

"It's an order," Fust growled. "We didn't bring you here for nothing; you must know that." He walked across the courtyard and Hugo had to follow, thinking Fust would never stop. Finally they were only thirty feet away from the doomed man.

The soldiers chained the young man to iron hoops in the wall. Blood trickled from the side of his mouth. One minute his eyes were popping hatred, every muscle taut. Then the fire went out of his eyes and he relaxed and looked around at everyone, reflective, and up at the sky, crinkling his eyes.

"It's a nice day," he said. And then, "Someone tell my mama I said good-bye."

The officer stepped back, leaving the young man alone. Realization came back to him, and the fire to his eyes, and he struggled wildly with the chains.

"I'll see you in hell, by God I will."

"Ready!" the officer said. The soldiers raised their guns.

"Take aim."

Hugo looked away.

"Fire!" The gunfire reverberated in the stone courtyard. The screaming of startled crows was the only sound that followed.

"Look at him, damn you," Fust said at Hugo's shoulder.

He was hanging limp from the chains, his head lolling forward, a pool of blood forming in the sand. Hard to believe that he called this a nice day just moments ago.

"I'm disappointed to see you're squeamish," Fust said.

Two soldiers dragged the young man's body away. Two others poured sand over the dark blood by the wall.

No one moved to disperse, and it was soon clear why. Shouted orders could be heard again inside. The big doors were thrown open. Two more soldiers led out a little man in black. The gold cross hanging around his neck told Hugo he was a bishop. He was probably in his late sixties, and fragile, with a cobweb of veins showing in his face. His black soutane was shabby, a streak of dust on it. He showed neither fear nor hatred, walking between the two soldiers, almost as Hugo had seen other bishops in procession, years ago, in the old cathedral.

In the absolute silence they brought him to the wall. Then the bishop said something to the officer, who eventually made a mocking bow. The bishop approached the firing squad, so close that Hugo could hear him when he spoke. He held out his hand to the first soldier.

"Don't be afraid," he said, "it is not your fault."

The soldier hesitated, then took the bishop's hand, his face carved in stone and looking away into the distance.

The next soldier was young, his face flushed and his eyes shifty. The bishop again held out his hand.

"Oh, Jon, I'm sorry to see you here. But how were you to know?"

The young soldier nodded dumbly, tears streaking his fresh face.

"Say good-bye from me to your father and mother." And then suddenly the bishop embraced him, the soldier responding with one arm, holding his gun with the other until it clattered to the cobbled courtyard.

"Enough!" It was the man from Moscow.

"That's Moscow speaking," Fust said in a conspiratorial voice to Hugo. "That roly-poly little bastard is Moscow. Never forget that."

The officer barked another order, and two soldiers moved quickly to lead the bishop back to the wall and tie him with the chain. The officer approached with a black band but the bishop declined it. He held the gold cross up in a gesture of benediction to everyone in the courtyard. The officer grabbed the cross and threw it violently into a far corner. It was not the cross, Hugo thought, nor the blessing: the officer was searching for a reason to be angry and brutal.

"Don't be timid this time," Fust said. "His name is Illyes — you may have heard of him?"

"No, sir."

"A renegade, my boy, that little runt is a renegade bishop. He had a chance to reform, but as you can see he is pig-headed to the end."

Hugo dared not turn away. He focused on the soldier whom the bishop had embraced. He felt sorry for the young man, his own age, disarmed by the bishop's kindly gesture and memories of a more tranquil past.

"Get ready," the officer shouted.

The young soldier prepared himself at attention like the others. At the order to take aim he raised his gun, but it was quivering visibly. For a brief instant Hugo glanced at the bishop. He was looking away at the sky, the veins still visible on his face. He must have visited here in happier days when the monks were free and young men were ordained amid the odor of incense.

The time was so long between the order to aim and the order to fire. The bishop might be looking at the sky, but his thoughts had to be with the bullets that would come screaming death. Hugo guessed that the young soldier's aim was not on the bishop. If someone missed, would they have a way of knowing who?

The courtyard reverberated again with the sound, and again the crows went hysterical overhead. The puffs of smoke from the guns hung in the air. The young soldier's gun was smoking too. At last Hugo forced himself to look at the body of the gentle little man who waved his tragic cross in forgiveness, now folded in the reddening sand.

Suddenly sick, Hugo ran off to the corner of the courtyard, where he vomited, supporting himself with one hand against the old stone wall. As he struggled to catch his breath, he was surprised to hear further sputtering on his left. Just a few feet away, the man from Moscow was having the same gastronomical problem. Life was a series of surprises.

Hugo was aware of the others observing him, even the despicable man from Moscow. They were making up their minds about him. The soldiers were dispersing. At least there would be no more killing that day.

"Time to eat," Ivoski said heartily.

Chapter Two

Summer flowers were lavish outside the sunlit dining room of the old monastery. Ivoski and the man from Moscow were on one side of a big wooden table, Hugo on the other. The man from Moscow muttered as he swatted at flies.

On the table were bottles of water and beer, plates of food. The man from Moscow poured himself a little water and sipped it. Ivoski was already guzzling beer and eating heartily. Through the window Hugo could see, beyond the flowers, soldiers shoveling sand where the executions had taken place.

"I hate executions," Ivoski said, wiping his mouth with the back of his hand.

Fust entered, toweling his head as if he had just taken a shower. He was full of energy.

"I hate executions, Hugo," he said. "The only one I know who enjoys executions is Ivoski here. What's the matter, boy? Aren't you hungry? Ivoski is such a pig. The trouble with you, Ivoski, is that you're a pig."

Fust, too, sat on the opposite side of the table, the towel now draped around his neck. He poured himself a beer, broke off a chunk of bread, and made the motions of preparing to eat like a pig, but he ate very little. Hugo could already see how unpredictable Fust was.

"Tell me now, Hugo," he said, "were you outraged? Did you want to run away? Or maybe run to the rescue, huh?"

"I didn't think about it that way."

"I'll tell you one thing about it for sure, Hugo — when all is said and done, it's better to be on the dishing out end than the receiving end. Am I right? You're damn right I'm right." He paused to observe Hugo. "Well, were you outraged, boy?"

"Well, the first one may have deserved it. But the bishop . . ."

"Ah, the bishop. What about the bishop?"

"He didn't seem dangerous or anything." Hugo was at a loss. "You could have put him in jail."

"But he is in jail, Hugo."

"I don't understand, sir."

"Look — I know he's not in jail, and you know he's not in jail, but no one out there knows one damn thing. If they knew, they'd make a martyr of him and go on pilgrimages and cause trouble."

"Then why did you kill him?"

"Because he was guilty."

Hugo could feel Ivoski's unforgiving eyes on him. The world was spinning much too fast, had gone out of control since morning in the mountains. There could be no rancor in that little bishop. Even after three years of Communist education it was hard to shake off the respect in which bishops were held. Golden-mitered once a year at Confirmation, they had carried ornate episcopal croziers that seemed too heavy to bear, the organ playing, time of incense, a cathedral of song, the spirit hovering and holy, the bishops wearing funny little satin shoes and administering a symbolic stroke on the cheek that allegedly made one a soldier of Christ. There was irony as well as sorrow. Ivoski saw that Hugo might faint and poured another glass of water. Hugo wanted to gulp it all but kept a little; he might need it more urgently later.

Fust, in his element, moved closer to Hugo.

"But seriously — it's because he wouldn't listen to reason. He was what we call a fanatic. They have no outward strength, no armies, you see, so they make up for it on the inside. With willpower. The other young man was nothing to fear; even you could see that. Then why did we execute him? you ask. Because if we didn't do it now we'd have to do it later. He'd have gone home to the mountains and boasted about how he fooled us, and then he would have caused further mischief, and eventually we would have to get rid of him. The bishop was another story. It didn't matter that the bishop couldn't prove he was right; we couldn't prove he was wrong either. So, for the people's sake, we had to kill him."

"What the bishop needed was a woman," Ivoski said with a leer, eating from a bowl of fruit.

Fust had been leaning forward intently but now jumped up and in an instant was at Ivoski's side. He slapped Ivoski on the back, a comradely gesture, then took Ivoski's bowl of fruit and threw it in the garbage.

"You're a pig, Ivoski, a fucking pig," Fust said. "We're making history here, so could you not slow down for a minute, you fucking pig?"

Fust returned and sat down. Ivoski might have been a pig, but Fust's real purpose was to give Hugo time to think and perhaps a chance to grab his life by the scruff of the neck and shake it and maybe begin to shape it into a Communist masterpiece for the future. The face the versatile Fust now presented was that of the man of destiny. But still Hugo was only a boy and raw, not to mention afraid. The man from Moscow seemed bored, chewing a fingernail. Back in the mountains, Hugo thought, they would now be playing soccer, the day's drill over, the sun and the mountain air in their faces, freedom.

"Why are you telling me this?"

"Because we want you to become a priest."

Images crowding. Priests climbing mountain roads on ancient bicycles, one a dark man like a blacksmith, the poor people going on their knees because, they said, he was carrying the body of Jesus. Dark face and long dark soutane — they begrudged him money but always called him when someone was dying or in other trouble, purple stole around his neck in the rain at funerals, shaking hands and never smiling, asking questions at school causing fear, cracked paint on the windows of his old house with the old housekeeper at the door, Veronica, scolding people for disturbing him, he himself pulling the rope for the Angelus bell when Veronica died.

Hugo was once his friend but avoided him when the war was being lost and others were saying that religion was for fools and the enemy of progress until Hugo despised him on his humble bicycle and finally denounced him at a meeting two years ago, although no one listened — no one would let anyone touch him because he had the power that only priests have.

"I don't understand, sir."

"We can't shoot them all, Hugo," Fust said. "They're spread throughout the population. The best way to reach them is from within."

"You're out of your mind, sir." Before he had finished saying the words, Hugo realized how out of line they were, especially considering how easily people could get shot. "My God, sir, I'm sorry."

"Son of a bitch, son, it's the first time today you were honest with me. And I'm grateful for that. There's just one thing — you may get as honest as you wish, but never, son, never tell me I'm out of my mind. Do you hear me? Because, unlike that old bishop, my mind is all I've got."

"But I'm at university, sir."

"We're not going to force you, Hugo. This undertaking is so great, the sacrifices so great, the dangers so great, it has to be a volunteer, someone who puts the Communist cause before everything else."

When he was thirteen Hugo wanted to be a priest. Most Catholic boys did. To be holy because only heaven mattered in the end. To hold up the little white bread, the body of Jesus, while the bell rang at the center of the world. To bring God and hope to old Maria dying next door. And keeping your own skin safe from the flames of hell. Nothing could compare. Until he was older and the boys would talk at school. That maybe it was not true. That maybe old Maria had no hell to fear or heaven to hope for, that it was all garbage taught by the priests to get people's money. And stories, too, about an old priest who had a housekeeper who was not what he said she was, his cousin, this twisted priest guzzling from the whiskey bottle and abusive on the altar on Sunday.

Then one day Hugo and the dark priest clashed. He came to the school and confronted the young renegade. "I hear you have been say-ing things about the church," he said. He forced Hugo to repeat the allegations, dragged them out of him. And when Hugo couldn't prove them, the priest hit him, knocked him down on the classroom floor in his black fury.

Hugo's comrades sat at their wooden desks disappointed because Hugo could prove nothing against the church and because he was not yet a big enough hero to hit the priest back.

It took just such a small incident to kindle into a conflagration the ember of distrust and even hatred for the church.

Later, at the university and enlightened, Hugo accepted that priests knew no better. They were victims of their own myths but no less dangerous for that. A way would have to be found to stop them. At the university it was only talk and games, but this now was life and ruthless and unimaginable choices.

"But it would take years of study, sir."

"It would take more than that, boy." Fust jumped to his feet again, began pacing. "It would take the rest of your life. Pay attention now. A priest is a priest forever. I'm sure you've heard that. Once you undertake this mission, there is no turning back, no other ambitions, no other work, no wealth or fame — are you following me, Hugo?"

Hugo sat dumbfounded.

"No marrying," Fust went on. "No women. Now are you following me? Never." Fust sat down, leaned across the table, intense. "Because we would want our priest to be the best in the country. The best who ever lived. Above suspicion. An example and inspiration, winning the people's affections, learning their secrets, learning how they think. Not for a few years but until the day he dies. That and nothing less."

"Don't just sit there, you dumb shit," Ivoski now said to Hugo. "It's a great honor to be asked."

This drove Fust into a tantrum real or feigned. He jumped up and turned on Ivoski.

"I should kill you, you horse's ass." He stood a moment fuming, then went to a sideboard, took out a handgun. "I'd be doing you a favor if I killed you, before someone else does it who will probably torture you first for being a horse's ass."

He whirled and flung the gun on the table in front of Hugo.

"Here! You do it, Hugo. It was you he insulted. Go on, be my guest. . . ."

For long moments the gun sat there, the short road to quick results in contrast with the interminable road Hugo was being asked to travel. All breathing stopped in the room, everyone waiting, the others looking at Hugo, Hugo looking at the gun. But Hugo made no move.

"Thanks, son, you'll make a good priest," Ivoski said when he saw he was safe.

The man from Moscow came around and picked up the gun and threw it in the garbage where Fust had thrown Ivoski's fruit.

"Sorry, son," Fust said. "These are trying times. We're all a bit on edge, huh?"

"I'd never get away with it. They know I'm in the Party."

"Nonsense. They believe in miracles. Don't you remember the story of the Prodigal Son. They'd welcome you with open arms, no questions asked." Fust now sat beside Hugo, pleading, his hand on Hugo's arm.

"But they'd find out eventually."

"Never. You're an actor, Hugo. After a while it would come naturally, like in the play." Now Fust talked like a proud father. "It will be the best-kept secret in the country, in the entire world. No one else will know, with the exception of the prime minister; yes, the prime minister will have to be told."

Hugo had dreamed for two years of doing something remarkable for the Party, making his mark, a place in the history books, the only real permanency — books would remain even after stone monuments were gone.

"I can't do it, sir," were the words that came out.

Fust jumped up, furious again, gesticulating.

"By God, you'll do it. You're not an imbecile, surely. What the Party wants, that is what you do...."

"No." It was the man from Moscow. He was looking away at the wall, sullen or sleepy or bored at having to arbitrate such petty bickering. "No," he repeated in a whisper. There was a long, pregnant pause. Then Fust retrieved the gun from the garbage, put it back in the drawer, turned to Hugo.

"You need time, son. It's a big decision."

Hugo hoped they would take him back to the mountains for the night, away from Fust, free to think in the cool breeze with the stars dancing above. He would have told no one, elevated above them all by his awesome secret and an offer unique in the history of the world. From such an eminent height he would have looked down on their youthful horseplay. Back in the mountains he would make a free choice.

They put him instead in a sprawling room with cracked plaster and brown water in a cracked jug sitting in a blue enamel basin. He could make no decision there, he thought feverishly, a picture of Lenin on the wall looking down and defying him. Fatigue engulfed him. He would decide in the morning.

He awoke in the middle of the night, nightmare and sweat, the little bishop looking at the sky and blue puffs of smoke coming from the guns. He would be alone if he became a priest; only four would know, all the others out to get him, puffs of smoke from other guns some frosty morning, the little man from Moscow no longer present to grunt "no" and save him.

He pulled on his clothes, tied his boots around his neck, and padded down the creaky corridor. He would hide in the mountains, cross the border, lose himself until they forgot him.

He emerged into the shadows of the courtyard. He pulled on his boots. He moved stealthily in the shadows from one pillar to the next.

"Couldn't sleep, boy?" Fust emerged from the shadows ahead. No escape. He knew; of course he knew. "I couldn't sleep either." He probably never slept, Hugo now thought. Fust had foreseen that Hugo would commit this act of weakness. Fust was unbeatable. He was the Party moving irrevocably forward to destiny, the puny, average people like Hugo falling limp by the wayside on the road to utopia where the history books would be written.

"I was just going for a walk," Hugo said lamely.

"How about a beer? I know where they keep the beer."

So they sat together at a small table in the kitchen where the only light was a candle that threw erratic shadows. After several drinks, Fust was loose and expansive. "Look at it this way, Hugo. No matter which side wins, you can't lose."

"I always had this dream of doing something great, though I never could figure out what it might be."

"Drink up that beer, for God's sake."

"We used to have this priest at home." Hugo was loose too. "He always looked like he needed a shave. I swear to God that man was my hero." Hugo held out his glass mug, which Fust unsteadily refilled.

"Then, at the university, I began to learn the true way of things, so when I went back to my village I didn't show proper respect. One Saturday, the priest came down the street on his old rusty bicycle. He threw down that old bike. Then he belted me. It was bad."

"He beat the shit out of you." Both Hugo and Fust were now quite drunk, both laughing inappropriately and swaying.

"He did. He beat the shit out of me. But I vowed to get him back."

"Yeah! Son of a bitch."

"Son of a bitch," Hugo repeated. "And now I'm going to do it. Yes, sir, son of a bitch."

Fust stretched out his hand, and they shook hands across the table.

"Of course he'll never know that you got him back. It's our secret, remember?"

"That's right, by God." Then the inebriated Hugo had a far-fetched thought. "But he'll find out in heaven. Think of it — he arrives in heaven and finds he has been one-upped all along by Hugo. Am I right? Am I right?"

"Time you were in bed, you big ox."

Fust stood up unsteadily, and Hugo followed suit, then staggered. Fust held him up, both laughing. As Fust held Hugo, they danced around in a brief drunken dance until Hugo knocked over the candle, which went out, leaving them in greater darkness.

"There's just one problem, you big ox: there's no heaven anymore, so your priest is never going to know you got the better of him."

"If he lives long enough, the bastard might read it in the history books." They shuffled out of the kitchen, still incoherent and laughing.

"Yeah, the history books, you're headed for the history books, you big ox. I love you already, you big fucking ox."

Chapter Three

Beyond the window of the rhythmically rattling train was the river Danube, majestic and tireless artery. There was a barge in the middle of the river, its black shoulders just above the water line. The barge, like the train, was turned away from the mountains and Hugo's home.

The train was nearly empty. The pulse of life was still slow since the war. People were not going places unless they had to, least of all on trains, the common memory still vivid of crammed carloads of shrunken, dumb, wide-eyed victims shuttled to the camps and death.

On the opposite seat sat Hugo's two cheap suitcases, a bag of hope and a bag of despair. His mother had gone with him to buy the black suit, in awe of him already. When the purchases were made, they stopped at the church where she thanked God for bringing him back from Communism to the bosom of the church. The red sanctuary lamp hanging before the altar winked and mocked him saying: I know about you.

The river turned a bend, and the railway followed it. There in the distance was the town of Dunauvaros, not very big, set against trees turning russet. It was September, time for the seminary. Hugo's heart had settled since he said good-bye to home, but now it jumped again. The time of trial was at hand.

Steam filled the red-brick station up to the dirty glass skylight, which had somehow escaped the war. The shouting of people was drowned by the engine hissing. Everyone was met by someone except Hugo, sweating, wearing his heavy black overcoat.

In his letter of acceptance the priest — Father Ladislaus — had given directions. In the letter, he'd been friendly and had said he was looking forward to having Hugo at the seminary. Hugo now felt conspicuous in the black suit. Everyone knew what it meant. Old women looked at him as his mother did, gladness in them that the faith and the church were still alive after everything that had happened. Hugo cursed inwardly, not them but the stupidity that would not let them free. They believed against all the evidence in a religion that mired them in guilt and kept them in subjugation with promises that offered infinitely more in the next life than in this one. Bitter amusement grabbed Hugo: he was living proof of how easy it was to fool them. Turn the other cheek and they believed he was a saint, while he meanwhile was out to scuttle them. It would be hilarious were it not for his own family being duped like all the others.

The street was busy in the early afternoon. Nearby, the cathedral steeple tapered to a tiny point in the sky. Turn right at the church, the priest had written. Hugo marveled at the cool head that had once placed the cross so high on the steeple. Later, he rested at a corner, not sure which way to turn. A group of young men loitered there. They turned their attention on him.

"Look, another man of God!"

"Say, there, priest, you forgot your skirts." Hugo looked at them defiantly. Just for a moment. It was what he would have to do for the rest of his life: adjust. Hide who he was. His role was as a seminarian. Tomorrow he would be wearing the long skirts, his soutane, and praying. He became meek and humble, smiling.

"I'm looking for the seminary, please."

"This is now a Communist town, you dumb shit."

"Not all of it." Hugo couldn't help a modest flare of defiance. Sweaty shirt wet and cold against his back, he picked up the heavy cases to get away from them.

"Don't go yet, holy man." A big youth blocked his way, the leader, others moving to the leader's side.

Hugo put down the cases. Other people were now gathering: men with nothing to do, always happy to see a fight; but others too, especially women with babushkas on their tired gray heads. He could see they pitied him, the raw seminarian; that was hardest to take. A little voice kept saying to him, you're from the mountains; you could beat the shit out of all of them one at a time or all together. He would leave the leader until last, kill him and his lazy, arrogant look. Then he would turn and run, leaving his bags behind, leaving the seminary behind, running to the edge of the world or until he fell, whichever came first, happy as he went down that he did not bow to these turds, consoled for ever, in whatever concentration camp they took him to, by the surprise and intense pain he would have inflicted on this interfering bastard.

"Say a prayer for us, priest."

"I'm not a priest."

"Don't contradict me, priest."

"Please." Hugo was meek now, not looking the young man in the eye, the new suitcases looking so ridiculous and prim on this crazy and violent street. Easy, he admonished himself: How could you have thought such mutinous thoughts so soon, you who just promised Fust everything, even your life? Some day these thugs would read about him in the history books — if they ever learned to read — and be ashamed that they stepped in the way of Hugo, elite and a hero, doing the unthinkable for his country when utopia was still only a dream.

"I won't ask you again, little girl," the leader said. "Start praying."

"Our Father, who art in heaven, hallowed be thy name..."

"Louder! Don't whimper like a girl, priest. Raise your voice and say it like a man."

"Thy kingdom come, thy will be done." Hugo kept his head high, the voice now loud and clear. Don't think about the words or the crowd, he told himself. Look at the cathedral with its steeple to the sky; think of the man who placed the cross on that dizzy steeple, above everything, like you, above them all. If they only knew, they would make you a hero. The words of the prayer were unfamiliar these many years.

"And lead us not into temptation," a little woman joined in, metallic clear. She wore a black scarf on her head. She was quickly pushed by one of the rowdy kids. She fell so easily. Her puffed, varicose leg showed blue blotches. Yet she had courage to defy everyone. Hugo was drawn between admiring and despising her. Look away and up, his inner self said, look above the fray. "But deliver us from evil, amen," he finished loudly and even proudly.

The young men clapped and hooted derisively. "Well done, priest; you pray like a girl."

"May I pass now?" Hugo picked up his cases with immense determination.

"Go in peace, my son," the leader mocked and stood aside with a bow. Fix his face in your mind, Hugo told himself. For some future day forty years from now when you can take revenge, after you have first made him feel rotten when you tell him what an exalted mission you were on that day on which he had the audacity to tangle with you.

"God bless you," the old woman said, but Hugo looked straight and high. She struck too close to home, could as well be his mother. The hurt in him was wide and deep, including father and brother for that matter. Everyone, he told himself, had to suffer in some different way before the world would be whole again. The buzz of excitement continued behind him. Already I am stirring things up, he thought, though he would have preferred to stir them some other way.

He passed shops and neat townhouses with polished plaques by the doors. People were going about their business. He absorbed every-thing — this was the world he would be leaving for six long years. He put down the cases to rest, wiped his face with a handkerchief.

Then, across the street, he observed in a doorway the lithe figure and haunted face of Zoltan Fust. Their eyes met for a moment. There was no flicker of recognition. Fust lit a cigarette and walked away quickly in the opposite direction.

Panic came rolling in: Hugo had come so close to wrecking his new life before it had even begun. For some moments he stood there, a statue. Then all the warnings came back, about carefulness and secrecy and playing the part. This too was the game, testing his composure at the eleventh hour when his will would be weakest before burying itself for six years. At least one thing, he thought: now Fust knows I'm an actor; I bowed in meekness, like a good seminarian; I passed that test.

Up the hill toward the seminary, two roads converged. Hugo could see in the distance another young man in black, carrying two big suit-cases like his own; it could mean only one thing. He felt a small, vague wave of contempt for this stranger he had never met.

The young man slowed down so that they would have to meet. It was pointless to try to avoid him: they would soon be locked up together for the years ahead. Fust's words pulsated in his head: he would not be pretending; he would be one of them.

"I'll carry yours if you'll carry mine," the young man said.

"What's the point?"

"Just a thought. The Lord said we should carry each other's load — something like that."

"That's not what he meant."

"Just a thought." The young man picked up his own cases and be-gan the steep climb to the seminary. He was about Hugo's age, wiry, his hair cropped short, a rubber face that would be hard to read. Hugo followed a step behind him to observe, obsessed with being stealthy and on his guard.

"What's your name?"

"Jeno. What's yours?"

"Hugo." He was determined he would not stop until the other did. But Jeno did not stop, went on and on, with surprising stamina, the big gray building seemingly far away as ever, like a mountain peak that seems to recede the more one climbs. Jeno talked out of the side of his rubber mouth. "It's my first time. Is it yours?"

"Yes."

"Good. Maybe we'll be friends."

Not if you don't stop soon for a rest — Hugo felt that Jeno was challenging him; his arms were bound to be aching too.

"Saint Joseph," Jeno pointed at a statue. The trees were beautiful and yellow in September's waning sun, and from the trees the stone statue looked down on the city. Jeno set down his cases in front of it. Maybe he was not aware of any contest, after all. If he kneels to pray I'll puke, Hugo thought.

"My father could do better," Jeno said, looking at the statue.

"He could like hell."

Jeno stared at Hugo for a long time. It wasn't clear if the stare was a challenge or if Jeno was trying to figure something out. Finally, he stretched out his hand and they shook.

"Hugo what?"

"Ovath. Hugo Ovath."

"He made a statue of Lenin for Debrecen Square. My father did."

"You're pulling my leg."

"My father is a Communist." This left Hugo without a ready answer. "But my mother is a Catholic." He stooped to pick up his cases. "They get along very well; you'd be surprised."

"Here, we'll try it your way," Hugo said. "You take mine and I'll carry yours." It was impossible to know people until one talked to them, and even then it was difficult. He was amused as well as surprised to find that Jeno's cases were heavier than his own. "What are you carrying here — bricks?"

The seminary loomed ahead, black figures moving about, the moment he had feared. There was, for a moment, a great sinking feeling of being totally alone. There was so much living to be done before his name could appear in the history books, and so much pretending. It was easy to be a hero back in the mountains — but what did they know about life?

"Know anyone here?" Jeno asked.

"No."

"I hope they're not a crowd of sanctimonious old farts. I don't suppose they'd allow girls."

"Are you totally crazy?"

"I was wondering if they'd object if my girlfriend came to visit."

"You're bullshitting me about having a girlfriend." Hugo was not amused.

"I suppose I am. But I had one until yesterday. Hope these old farts are right and there's a God; otherwise I'm getting a raw deal, I can tell you."

"But didn't she try to stop you? And you — what the hell is the matter with your head?" Hugo could not hide his amazement that someone would give up a genuine girl for a life like this.

"Sure, she tried to stop me. She's in the Party, too, so naturally she says there's no God. Neither of us could prove it either way, so here I am."

Their climb over, their new leather shoes crunched the dry gravel. Flowers were neatly tended in beds of several shapes. A fountain to the side had run dry. No doubt it had a history, which could be the history of the church or the country: some said that one had run dry and some said the other.

Another seminarian and his rich parents were getting out of a car, a high-shouldered lad with heavy glasses. Hugo took an instant dislike to him — he should have come on a donkey's back if what they claimed was true. He would take note of this young capitalist. Meanwhile, he resisted the urge to ask Jeno more about his girl despite great curiosity about how she said good-bye. Images jumped to mind of lips slightly open, hips curved out, a girl's body bent forward. Hugo had never for all his bravado pressed against the body of a girl. How could Jeno give it up without having Fust to persuade or bully him?

"And who have we here?" The priest who came to meet them was about forty. He was sallow and untidy, ashes on his black soutane and a pipe at arm's length in his left hand while his right stretched ahead of him in greeting. They told him their names.

"You're welcome indeed. I'm Father Ladislaus, the rector. I know

we'll get along famously. You're welcome. Or did I say that already?"
He was expansive and transparently glad to see them and hoped they
had a pleasant trip. He took two of their cases, in spite of their polite protestations, and led the way inside, down long corridors, with
pictures of bishops and saints on the walls. Upstairs, he showed them
two little adjacent rooms.

"Your cells," he said.

"I'm so glad you're here," he said quietly to Hugo when they were
alone. It might be a special message or it might mean nothing. Hugo
presumed his parish priest would have told the rector about his wandering from the fold and then returning. Fust was right. They loved
Prodigal Sons and asked no questions, taking miracles for granted.

There were a bed, a table, a chair. And a plaster cross on the wall.
"Supper will be at seven," Father Ladislaus told Hugo as he left.

There was an hour to spend. He unpacked his cases, hanging his
scant supply of clothes from nails on the walls. With a mixture of
intrigue and trepidation he put on the black soutane, fastened the row
of little buttons down to his feet. He attached the white plastic collar. It was tight and uncomfortable, but worst of all was the shame.
He was dressed like a woman, in skirts. He was embarrassed to meet
Jeno, whose rubber face might laugh, never mind that Jeno and the
others would be dressed in the same catastrophic way. There was no
mirror to show him how it looked. He wanted to go next door and
get the embarrassment over. It might help form some useful alliance
with Jeno. He couldn't live as an adrift island for the duration of his
priestly life. And each time a big unaccustomed concept like priestly
life came into view, he wanted to run like hell from a predicament
that had deprived him of most of the best things on earth before he
even got a chance to savor them.

Anyway, it was against the rules to visit Jeno's room. There was no
sound except occasional footsteps in the creaky wooden corridor. He
knocked on the wall, and Jeno's knocking answered him, a friendly
though slightly mocking sound.

In the long, cold refectory there were a flagstone floor and wooden
rafters and a painting of the Last Supper on the end wall. Hugo
guessed there were about sixty students, and eight priests at the head
table with Ladislaus in the middle.

Some of the students were surprisingly old, their hair thin or
gone. Six years of study and prayer took their toll; it showed in their

strong-jawed granite faces. Hugo had expected to despise them, their manhood hidden under the so-called skirts, but it wasn't so easy to dismiss them. Some no doubt had fought in the war. Some were probably heroic. They were the kind who would challenge death without thinking, believing themselves ready to die and go to their reward, like Bishop Illyes.

Or maybe they said good-bye to a girl years ago, as Jeno did yesterday. They must be strong bastards to survive the hankering and longing, living this Spartan life in order later to fix the broken world with the help of such flimsy instruments as hope and love.

They stood in an untidy line while Ladislaus said, in Latin, the grace before meals: "Benedic, Domine, nos, et haec tua dona quae de tua largitate sumus sumpturi, per Christum Dominum nostrum," to which they all answered an eager "amen." As they sat to eat, a seminarian stood and read from the *Imitation of Christ*, by Thomas à Kempis. "Every time I go among men I return less a man," he read, a bleak picture of their common rocky road and destiny.

The food was hauled in on a two-tier trolley. It was Friday, so there was fish. The priests at the head table were served first. Hugo was near the bottom with the other newcomers. Soon, no one was listening to Thomas à Kempis, everyone silently making signs to everyone else to pass the milk or bread but seldom the unsavory fish.

After a while Ladislaus tinkled a little bell. He welcomed the seminarians back from summer vacation and thanked God for the new recruits. Don't thank God, Hugo thought wryly, thank Fust and the despicable Ivoski. Ladislaus sat down, and conversation dominated the remainder of the meal.

"My name is Miklos," the newcomer on Hugo's right said. He was a small, mousy lad with glasses.

"And mine is Hugo." After that they did not know what to say. Two places away, the young man who had arrived by car was telling anyone who would listen that his name was Antal and his father was a writer and they lived in a house with seventeen rooms. Several of the others were listening politely, relieved of the burden of having to talk themselves, but Hugo was sure that within a month they would put the brazen Antal in his place.

"Do you like music?" Miklos asked.

"Yes, I suppose so."

"Do you play an instrument?"

"No. I really don't know much about music." He hoped Miklos would lapse into silence. Finding common ground for conversation would be a challenge. Jeno caught his eye and raised his mug in a secret toast. Antal was saying he had been a member of the national soccer team. That and chess were his passions. And philosophy. It was a relief when Ladislaus tinkled the little bell and set them free.

The students walked in big or small groups outside, out-shouting one another to tell about their summers. Hugo and Jeno conspired to walk together. Both homesick, they further depressed themselves by talking about their families.

"But the joke, Hugo — know what the ultimate joke is? Look at us. We should be out chasing women."

"You need to watch your tongue, Jeno."

"No sex for the rest of your life, my friend — it's sort of crazy when you think about it." It struck Hugo that he had thought more about sex in a few hours in the seminary than he had for months on the outside when there were other challenges to occupy his mind.

An old priest joined them. He had a thin, bent neck like a turkey. Father Gyula, he said. He held his hands behind his back and walked stooping forward, his voice low and hoarse.

"Are you homesick, boys?"

"A little, Father."

"I was too, sixty-one years ago. I almost went home that first night. A few times since then I was sorry I hadn't, but something kept me here, God I suppose." He looked at Hugo quizzically, making him feel uncomfortable — this was a man who maybe could read your mind. "I'll give you only one piece of advice: stay at least the first night. It will all look better in the morning."

It was so easy to be beguiled by this old man. If you spent enough time with him, Hugo thought with rising alarm, you might eventually blurt out every secret. And old Gyula would not be surprised or blame you — that was part of the beguilement. He resolved one more time to be forever vigilant.

"You two will be good friends," Father Gyula said before going inside. He had a way of making things sound prophetic and pre-determined, probably because of his great age, and the two were self-conscious as they followed him indoors.

The lights were dim in the long corridors, but they could still see the saints on the wall, Thomas Aquinas and Augustine and others.

And then the bishops, their names etched on little brass plates. Among them was a familiar face, that of the quiet and fearless bishop who stood looking at the sky before the bullets came screaming that awful morning only two months ago. The plaque said his name was Bishop Illyes.

He would be looking down at Hugo every day for the next six years, bringing back memories of the puffs of casual smoke from the guns, and his little smile. How was he to know it would end as it did? But he would have gone through life smiling anyway, Hugo thought with begrudging admiration.

"Do you know him?" Jeno asked at his shoulder.

"Him? No."

Chapter Four

Candles flickered on the altar; the flame fluttered in the red lamp over the sanctuary; the gold tabernacle shone — testimonies to God. It would be two hours yet to sunrise. They sat in black rows in the carved seats of the chapel and chanted the divine office. "By the rivers of Babylon, there we sat and wept when we remembered you, Zion." The words were thousands of years old, a Jewish legacy from the days before Jesus. They chanted in Latin, mysterious and threatening. It was overwhelming: How could Hugo ever cope with their centuries of mystery, how penetrate their secrets, win their confidence, learn their private language, defeat them? And all alone.

Sometimes they sat and sometimes stood, often bowing. Hugo struggled to keep up with the Latin, odd words remembered from school.

The divine office over, Father Gyula, flanked by two seminarians, came out to offer Mass. The Gregorian hymns rose and fell like waves on a great ocean, "Veni, Creator Spiritus, mentes tuorum visita." It was so magic and moved you so strongly, you could march out to death not caring. The Party had no songs to match it or lift you up like that.

The great ordeal drew closer — Holy Communion. He would have to leave his choir stall and go up there to the front and take the white bread on his tongue, which would be, under the circumstances, a sacrilege. Two years of mockery and cynicism could not eradicate all the years of believing. It was death to go if he had sinned, mocking God who loved him. God might stay silent and meek for now, and not strike him dead, but his day would come, Hugo's day of pain and death. It helped to keep telling himself there was no God and it was only bread, but a fear still gripped him. He could not approach the sacrament. But he could not stay away either. They would say nothing, but they would think and wonder; it might be the first in a series of clues that they would later string together around his neck.

He wore a heavy sweater under the long soutane, but it was still cold as ice in the September morning. He dreaded what it would be like in January. The others did not seem to notice. Years of this hardship were etched on their lean, tight faces. There was nothing in the Party to match their discipline and endurance. Their eyes were closed and their heads bowed for the consecration in a great stillness broken only by the ringing of the pure bell. The terrible moment came closer.

There was a commotion on the other side of the aisle, and then a thud. A student had fainted, one of the new ones. There was shuffling as three seminarians carried him out, one holding his feet as if pushing a wheelbarrow. For a moment Hugo thought of fainting too. It would get him out of this awful predicament. But he couldn't faint every morning. Maybe he would get lucky and be struck dead before this spiritual or psychological crucifixion, whatever it was, got out of hand.

"Lord, I am not worthy," the words rumbled through the full chapel. Nostalgia: happy days of youth before the war with father and mother and dressed special for Sunday and the dark-faced priest filling hearts with fortitude not to give up no matter what. If they were all so wrong then, where did the happiness come from? And if they were right, it was unhappiness and death to go up there today, an unbeliever, and take on his tongue the living piece of bread.

Gyula came down to meet them, holding the full silver ciborium in his knuckly hand, standing in the middle. The oldest went first, white stoles across their shoulders because they were deacons, one step short of priests, their heads bowed and thinking; so much thinking must have taken place behind their downcast eyes.

The rows moved steadily out and back. A low hymn rose. When it was time, Hugo got up in unison with the others in his row. The bread had the same dry, tasteless lightness as years ago. He felt nothing. No fear. No relief. No holiness. No ridicule. He had done it. It would be easier tomorrow. Soon, it would no longer be an issue. There would be other obstacles to cope with. His stomach was rumbling. He longed for breakfast.

They ate in silence. There were great dishes of porridge and pewter jugs of warm milk. The student who had fainted sat pale and unhappy, eating nothing. Outside the tall windows, darkness at last gave way to daylight. The days would be endless.

Out of the quietness a young man screamed at a table opposite, jumping to his feet. "Take it away," he was shouting. Ladislaus was quickly on the scene. A chair fell on its back.

"It's a mouse," the young man was shouting. "It was in my bowl." He pointed. "Take it away."

Ladislaus picked it up, a soft toy mouse, lifelike and revolting in the way the innocent mouse is said to be revolting.

"All right, who was it?" Ladislaus had not shaved. He looked tired.

"I did." Jeno's rubber face was straight, but already Hugo knew well that he was laughing inside as he stood there waiting for sentence.

"Did everyone have enough to eat?" Ladislaus asked finally. No one dared answer. "Good." Ladislaus put the mouse in his pocket. They did not yet know him well enough to be sure if the incident was over or a verdict merely postponed.

"Aristotle was born in Stagira in 384 B.C." The nervous priest went to the blackboard and wrote the place and date. "Write that down," he told them. They opened their fresh notebooks and wrote.

"He studied under Plato at the Academy of Athens...."

The priest had a smooth, unworn face. He never told them his name, and no one asked.

"Aristotle formulated the theory that everything in the world can be reduced to matter and form. Matter is the raw material. It is the possibility of form...."

They had no idea what he was talking about, but they wrote stray words in their notebooks and waited for illumination that never came. After an hour a bell rang deep in the building. The priest picked up his faded pages of notes and left at once.

Over by the window, Antal proceeded to explain matter and form to several students. They abandoned him one by one when they saw he knew nothing about it either. Hugo was sitting beside Jeno. When they got up to go, someone had tied the tail of Jeno's soutane to the desk behind. They already liked him.

Playing soccer was the one time he could be free as in the mountains. The newcomers played together, about twenty in all. They were joined by a couple of the younger priests. Time of sweat and mud and flashes of anger — you could relax, away from the bells and the scrutiny, away from the accusing picture of the murdered Bishop Illyes.

Because Antal had said he played on the national team, he was chosen first. A big priest named Mor was chosen second, a tribute to priesthood over talent, since no one knew who was good and who was not. In such a vacuum Antal was happy to take over and arrange everything.

The novices were too respectful to tackle the priests, except Antal, sliding feet first at Mor in the mud, Mor's pearly teeth bared in a smile of steely resolve as Antal glided away with the ball. He evaded one tackle, then another. He had plenty of time to pass to another player, but Antal, selfish, wanted to do it all alone until the ball trickled harmlessly away as a student hit him.

Ladislaus prowled the sideline, shouting and gesticulating.

When a goal was scored, it was the little student Miklos who scored it, doing nothing spectacular but standing around unobserved and taking his chance when it came.

Antal came forward again, face fiery red, others shouting for a pass and ignored. He eluded two blundering backs, and then there was only Jeno in goal who came out to meet him like a thundering rhino. Antal went down in a heap and Jeno went away with the ball.

Only one more goal was scored, and again it was Miklos taking his chance when it came.

Several students confronted Antal, who confessed that he was merely a substitute on the national team, and, yes, his father was a member of the selection committee.

When they returned to the seminary, it was surrounded by soldiers. Iron trucks with little windows were stationed at the entrances. Other soldiers roamed inside the building. An officer spoke quietly to Ladislaus, who scratched his untidy hair and brushed ashes from his soutane. The seminarians went inside.

Upstairs, the seminarians stood in whispering groups. When Hugo joined one such group it grew unaccountably quiet. It means nothing, he tried to tell himself.

There were shouted orders in the courtyard below. A stocky student was led away in handcuffs. Someone said his name was Joszef. He had served table at breakfast, bringing extra bread with a broad smile to the newcomers at the lower tables. The soldiers shoved him into a truck. The trucks droned and nosed their way down the avenue.

"You were a star," Hugo said to Miklos at dinner.

"I got lucky," Miklos said. But he knew about soccer and could recite an endless litany of famous players, including the mythical Stanley Matthews of England.

After dinner they walked again in groups through the lovely seminary grounds, and Ladislaus walked with them. He said the Party tried every trick to harass the church. He said the regime had stopped all funds, and the seminary was in financial straits.

"It's the fault of the Soviets, Father," a novice said. "They don't believe in God."

"Don't blame the Soviets," Ladislaus said. "It is our own weak people. They don't want to be poor, so they listen to whoever offers them more bread on the table."

"What did Joszef do wrong?"

"They say he spoke out against the Party during summer vacation."

"What will they do to him?"

"Nothing much. They will try to scare him. He will be back in a few days."

There was a letter from Hugo's mother, full of pride for Hugo's conversion and calling, but anguish too for his brother, Ferenc, two years younger, who had joined the Party and came home from meetings full of venom for his brother the traitor.

"Did you not get a letter?" he asked Miklos.

"My parents are dead." How could he love music, then, except perhaps the sad music for what was lost?

Confessions were on Saturday mornings. Hugo had no option but to go. The secret to survival was to be average: don't do less than the others, nor too much more.

Father Mor was in one confessional and Father Gyula in the other, their names printed on the doors of the wooden boxes in which they sat behind red curtains on velvet cushions. He chose the old man. Students were lined up and waiting, their backs to the wall, each withdrawn into his private world to wrestle with right and wrong and examine where life was taking him. Gyula's whisper rose occasionally to a mumble and faded again.

It had been so long, Hugo could scarcely remember the formula. "Bless me, Father, for I have sinned." But what sins were considered average in a place like this? If he knew, he would tell them to old Gyula and keep him happy and avoid suspicion. Sins grew in stature with the passing years. When he was young he told about fighting and name-calling, and then about the thoughts and stirrings that bothered him in the night. Was it reasonable to admit to such flesh and blood here? The others must sometimes think about women too. But just to be safe, he decided not to mention it, at least not yet.

There was the shuffle of someone exiting the box on the other side. Jeno emerged wearing on his head a fake pair of horns, like those of the devil. As he turned, they could all see his fake tail. With two forefingers he stretched his rubber mouth from ear to ear. The others laughed inwardly, but Jeno did not laugh. Was his life so uncomplicated and pure, Hugo wondered, that he had no fear?

When it was his turn, Hugo pulled the curtain behind him. He told Gyula it was a month since his last confession, the first lie. Then he confessed telling lies. And other minor sins from his youth. Then he told, in a burst of honesty, about his dislike for one of the novices.

"Would it be because this novice talks too much?"

"Yes, Father."

"A little boastfully maybe?"

"Yes, Father."

"And maybe because he comes from a rich family and is spoiled and had all the things you never had?"

"Could be, Father." The priest knew. Hugo did not have to mention Antal's name. There in the darkness the priest knew. Did he see other secrets? He asked no more questions, and Hugo followed the formula, saying he regretted all the sins of his life. Then he waited in the blackness.

"Did you come from a farm, son?"

"Yes, Father."

"Tell me, did you have pigs?"

"A few, Father."

"And a horse?"

"We had no horse, Father."

"Pigs are the most fascinating animals. They're so easy to please. And so incurious. Did you ever notice that?"

"I never paid much attention."

"I remember how they would sniff the wind. Apart from such odd moments they are very unreflective animals, not like cows, always brooding. Had you a mountain?"

"A lot of mountains, Father."

"We had a hill. I climbed it a thousand times." He paused a moment. "What would you like for your penance?"

"Whatever you say, Father."

"In that case, First Corinthians, chapter 13." He gave Hugo absolution in Latin, his old hand making a shaky sign of the cross beyond the wire screen. "Say a prayer for me, son. You may go now."

It was a shock to come out of the dark box to sunlight and reality. He felt no great load lifted as he once had felt on such occasions. It was only when conscience was tender that the lifting of the load brought relief. He hurried to his room to see what might be in chapter 13; it might be the key to something. But he could find no key.

"I may speak with every tongue that men and angels use, yet if I have no charity I am no better than echoing bronze or the clash of cymbals." Sure, it applied to his animosity for Antal, but was that all? "At present we are looking at a confused reflection in a mirror; then, we shall see face to face."

If he let loose his imagination he could make strings of connections, all different, but he could never be sure which was the right one.

Chapter Five

On a spring day he walked to the railway station to meet his parents and his brother Ferenc. He still felt uncomfortable in the long black soutane, which made him conspicuous, as if he were from Mars. People walked fast, going about their business. A platoon of soldiers embarked on a train. A girl kissed a young man good-bye. This was the life of the world passing him by.

His mother already looked smaller and older, embracing him with shining eyes of pride. His father slapped him on the back and laughed, nervous but excited. Ferenc remained at a hostile distance.

"You look lovely," his mother said, and he knew she was referring to the hated soutane.

"We'll be late for lunch unless we hurry." The parents walked on either side of him, Ferenc dragging behind. His father, usually garrulous and opinionated, was silent and hanging on Hugo's words.

"You lost weight," his mother said.

"I'm in good health."

Other students had visitors too. After lunch, Ladislaus fussed over them.

"And what about you, young man?" he said to Ferenc. "We have room for another Ovath."

"No, thank you."

In the strained silence the mother started to cry. "He's running around with the Communists," she said.

"Don't worry, Mrs. Ovath," Ladislaus consoled, at a loss. In the war she had hidden in bushes behind the hill, the two boys clinging to her. The Nazis took families away that were said to be disloyal; it could be a matter of life and death. After such a hard life she deserved some peace. Hugo knew no better way to cope than to blame his brother and silently hate him.

They walked in the lovely grounds in the afternoon.

"Maybe you could say a word to your brother," the father said behind the mother's back.

They met Jeno's parents. Hugo observed Jeno's father with respect, an artist and Party member, though he didn't look the part — a quiet man with hollow cheeks and bulging eyes. The two mothers talked like friends. Jeno showed Hugo a box, and when he opened it a rubber snake sprang out.

On the way back to the station, Hugo dropped back beside Ferenc.

"You could come home," his brother said. "You don't belong here."

"Sorry, Ferenc, this is where I belong."

"You'll rot in it."

Hugo wished he could go with them, begin life again, steer clear of causes — they cost too much. The summer would be hell.

Lent was the time of ashes and penance for forty days in spring, a reminder of the dust from which they came and to which they would return.

"You'll starve yourself to death; that's a sin too," Jeno said to Hugo.

"Don't worry." He would show them. Or at least himself. When the others took two slices of bread, he took one. He wanted to be satisfied that one did not need to believe in God or everlasting reward to be exceptional and make sacrifices.

One morning, Ladislaus asked them to pray for Father Gyula, who was ill. Hugo did what he had not done before: he prayed internally for old Gyula. He even wanted the prayers to be answered.

By Holy Week they were keeping vigil with Gyula, lest he die in the night. At midnight on Wednesday it was the turn of Hugo and Miklos.

"I'm sorry to keep you out of bed, boys." Hugo was surprised that he seemed so lively.

The room was as bare as those of the novices. There was no luxury, then, that came as a reward for seniority. Or as a sign of capitulation to the world's comforts. Gyula had survived like this for sixty-one years. He must have harbored some great hope, and maybe it did not matter whether it was well founded or not — all that mattered was that it sustained him.

"We're all praying that you'll be better soon."

"That's not how prayers work, son. I won't be getting better. Good Friday is the day I plan to go."

Good Friday was two days away.

The night hours passed slowly. The old man sipped water, his tongue caked. Then he dozed, one raised bony knee creating a tent of the blanket.

"What day is it?"

"Wednesday night, Father."

"When I was young we had a dog called Sailor, with a broken tail. He was a fighting dog. I remember a grass bank by a wall where he would lie at my feet on Sundays. Do me a favor, lads, and wake me if I fall asleep again."

"But you need the rest, Father."

"Rest doesn't matter now. When I sleep I dream of her looking over the wall. It was years before I realized what she wanted. Only thirteen but she knew, and I didn't. She still refuses to leave me alone."

All the time he was admonishing others behind the dark confession grille, she was at the back of his mind, the flesh hanging around him in sags and wrinkles, more than eighty years, and still the imagination was on fire and regrets standing on their hind legs and gnawing at him.

He was the only one who might have turned my head, Hugo thought. He could read minds in that confession box. He could be young and joking with the novices after sixty-one years, and he could give the impression that the life he lived was the most worthwhile ever lived and that the world and human clay were ultimately conquerable by the spirit. There was no one perfect, though. It was a matter of finding the best way to survive.

Miklos had gone to the kitchen. It was Hugo's chance to find perhaps a speck of sense, the only chance he might ever get. In a couple of days Gyula would be dead and Hugo out of harm's way.

"What if there's no God, Father?"

For a long time Gyula said nothing, and Hugo wondered if he had heard at all. There were stars outside the window, and he put on his thick glasses and seemed to be looking at them, maybe saying a sort of good-bye if he was planning to go on Friday.

"She was only thirteen and I was only fifteen. I heard years later that she married unhappily."

On Friday night they were all called to his room, most kneeling outside in the corridor and praying the Glorious Mysteries. The stars were still outside the window, but Gyula could no longer see them, in a coma now, the bony fingers around a rosary, a big candle by his bed to light him to heaven if there was a heaven and if he was ready to go there. And if he was not ready, no one was, sixty-one years thinking about that girl, no longer thirteen and smirking but older and sagging and maybe now dead. Hugo wished Gyula whatever reward he wanted, and after sixty-one years only an eternal reward seemed good enough.

The night was wearing on, and it looked as if he would be wrong about Good Friday, but he died before eleven, Ladislaus holding his hand and telling the others he was gone. Many students cried openly. Hugo was moved too, though he fought the tears, not having cried for a long time, since the death of his dog, a dog who'd belonged to his mountain days.

They buried Gyula in the little cemetery behind the chapel. He had no family left. If the girl of his dreams knew, who knows, she might have come and gladdened his heart at last. If she were still alive. Hugo was assigned to carry one of the candles in the procession to the grave, the wind extinguishing it and someone else lighting it, time for thinking, even Jeno solemn and playing no tricks. It mattered whether there was a heaven.

A letter arrived from Uncle Georg. Although Hugo knew about the ruse, it still gave him a jolt. The letter expressed the hope that Hugo was well and that he was making progress with his studies and his spiritual life. Uncle Georg wrote that he was glad to be back from his travels, without saying where he had traveled. He was looking forward to seeing Hugo on visiting Sunday, a week away.

Hugo had no Uncle Georg.

Zoltan Fust looked debonair wearing a red scarf as he drove at high speed up to the front door of the monastery. Hugo resented Fust's intrusion into the orderliness of his life and the precarious security he had established. The death of Gyula still hung over the seminary, not sad but peaceful and even triumphant. The time was wrong.

"Welcome, Uncle Georg."

"Hugo, my boy!" Fust embraced him warmly, taking Hugo by surprise. It was obvious Fust was enjoying the role. "You got my letter?" he said more quietly.

"Yes."

"Any problems?" He led Hugo back to the car, where he unloaded cakes and chocolates. He was in his element.

"No, sir."

"No, Uncle Georg. Where can we talk?"

"In the garden. But you'll have to meet Father Ladislaus."

"Naturally, my boy."

In the garden they sat on black iron chairs at an iron table and Hugo relaxed as he told Fust how smoothly things were going.

"I got the gold medal for philosophy. It turns out, I'm fairly smart."

"Not to mention a good actor."

"Thank you, Uncle Georg."

"Uncle Georg can pick them — am I right?"

"Don't look now, but here comes Ladislaus."

Ladislaus arrived with his arm out in welcome, pipe coming behind him in his left hand.

"So you're Uncle Georg?"

"None other, Father."

"And Hugo tells me you've been abroad."

"That's right. Haven't seen the boy for two years. How's he doing?"

"A fine young man, diligent and prayerful, he'll make a good priest."

"Excellent, excellent." Fust was such a knave, Hugo thought. Ladislaus moved away to the next group, waving, always waving. "Is he as naive as he seems?" Fust asked.

"He's a very fine man. They say he'll be a bishop one day."

For an hour Fust asked questions and Hugo answered. Then they went to Vespers in the chapel. Hugo sang loud and proudly; he'd let the bastard see what an actor he was. Afterward, he introduced Uncle Georg to Jeno and others. It was the normal thing to do. When it was time to depart, they walked down the long corridor toward the front door.

"You make me nervous, boy." Fust moved into his low, controlled voice.

"What do you mean?"

"You're so damn enthusiastic."

"You told me you wanted the best priest ever ordained."

"That I did, by God."

Fust stopped and looked up at the taller Hugo with a hint of admiration, gave him an encouraging pat on the arm.

When they reached the picture of the dead Bishop Illyes, Fust did not notice until Hugo pointedly stopped in front of it.

"What do they say about him?"

"Only that he's missing."

"If they knew he was dead they would build shrines to him. They're very stupid."

"No they're not, sir." Hugo blurted it out before he had time to think it over.

"Good God," Fust turned on him. "They've won you over."

He walked on briskly, his cocky head high, Hugo trailing. At the front door, he got into the car without a handshake.

"Sir?" Hugo said, and Fust looked up impatiently as he started the engine. "We could call it off." There was a long pause. "If you're nervous about it."

"And what would you do?"

"Don't know."

"Stay on and become a real priest?"

"I couldn't do that, sir. I don't believe in God."

"Only thing is — if we called it off, surely you can see the risk you would pose for the Party, knowing what you know?" He turned off the engine for emphasis. "We'd have to kill you." He started up the engine at once, waved to Hugo like a proud uncle, and moved down the avenue at high speed.

It was July and sunshine as the slow train struggled back to the mountains. Many of the passengers were returning home from the coal mines in the north, black on their faces that couldn't be washed away. Hugo listened to them talking about the events of the past year. The Party had consolidated its power. Rakos was the man of the moment. No one said what Hugo suspected, that it was a puppet government imposed by Moscow. The big Soviet army was standing by just in case. Final victory over the minds of the people was still a long way off.

Some were rowdy, downing bottles of cheap wine and talking about women. They were the people for whose loyalty everyone was fighting. Up from the mines, they wanted only their wives and children or even a woman without a name.

Hugo's heart leaped at last to the familiar mountains. He was superior to them now. He had traveled. His quiet parents were so happy and smiling at the railway station, his mother in her Sunday clothes, saying he must be tired from the journey when it was she who must be tired from life's ungenerous lot.

His father carried the big case two miles to the house. It looked like a doll's house after the big seminary. The leg of the kitchen table was still broken, and on the dresser the brown dishes his grandmother had given his mother, so drab and unimportant.

"We did up your room," his mother said.

"Where is Ferenc?" he asked at supper around the kitchen table.

"He went to that camp," his father said.

They would want him to do something. Already, after only one year. Maybe even work a miracle. It was unfair.

"It will do him no harm," was all he could think to say.

"How could it do him no harm?" The father's impotent anger exploded. "He has given up the church. He is angry all the time. If I was a younger man I'd throw him out."

"You must talk to him, Hugo," his mother said.

"I'll talk to him."

He went out to the little fields while there was still light, looking around vaguely for his carefree youth: in the round, weather-washed stones of the wall, the field of green wheat swaying, the seeds of which his father shook in hope and patience. A light was flickering in the house where Bela Kalman killed a man and then died. By the low wall were the flowers he knew, yellow despite the gathering darkness. He would wait until tomorrow to tell them that he too must go to camp for the summer.

"It's a special honor," he explained. "It's sponsored by the bishop." He had the lies neatly arranged.

Fust was there the day camp opened.

"Welcome, Hugo." But there was no hugging.

"Thank you, sir."

"I want you beside me at dinner."

"Me, sir?"

"You're special, boy. You'd better get used to being treated special."

There were about two hundred recruits in the camp, and he walked by them at Fust's heels to the table at the top, a hush in the room. They were first to be served, treated with respect by young men with squared shoulders. Lenin looked down from a wall.

Fust was not a chameleon for nothing. He put on his friendly face and plied Hugo with wine until he relaxed.

"Have you any regrets, Hugo?"

"No."

"I myself never could swallow all that mystery."

"May I speak freely, sir?" Hugo put down his knife and fork.

"I guess you'd better."

"Well, sir, there's nothing easier to swallow than the mysterious and incredible — so long as they don't ask you to understand it. Churches have kept people in line for thousands of years, sir, by asking them to believe things they can't understand..."

"Do you say things like this at the seminary?"

"Oh no, sir."

"Why did you become a Communist, Hugo?"

"The truth is, I can't explain it."

"Really?"

"A priest hit me one day, as I think I may have told you, sir. I think that's the real reason."

"It seems such a small, pissy reason, if you ask me. And what if they're nice to you again now — maybe you'll do another about-turn and believe all over again."

"Don't think so, sir."

"I don't follow you, son."

"That's what's mysterious, sir. There comes a time when talking is no good anymore."

"Are you pulling my leg?"

"No, sir. And you want to know why? I don't want to get shot; that's why I'm trying to be truthful as I can at all times."

Hugo realized he was having a good time, until he became aware that he was under observation from his fellow recruits.

Fust meanwhile talked on about his aimless youth. At times he seemed so human, drawing Hugo to him. He had been down, once, in the gutter, he said, and walked over. Then the Party was formed, and he found a cause. Hugo felt the power come back into him that the Party gave, power embodied in such as Fust, a man of destiny. It made a difference to be sitting there beside him, made Hugo feel strong and proud.

"That fellow, Antal, I'd keep an eye on him."

"What do you mean?"

"Don't get too friendly; that's all."

"I'm not." How could he even know Antal? Hugo had not bothered to introduce Antal to Uncle Georg. "He's just a bigmouth."

"The word is that you're very friendly with him."

The wine wore off at once, and Hugo's happy dinner went sour. It was stupid ever to feel that he was getting close to Fust. The bastard knew everything. He had spies there too. How else could he know? Maybe there were others in the same position as Hugo himself, impostors too. It was his fate in life that he could never trust anyone again. It would be useless to explain to Fust that he loathed the smug Antal but that Father Gyula, before he died, had persuaded Hugo in confession to try to like Antal and even love him, never mind that Hugo didn't even believe in confession.

"I'm just trying to help." The manipulating Fust changed gears again. "Just offering friendly advice, because I like you and don't want you to make mistakes."

From that dinner forward his peers were suspicious of Hugo. Still, it was glorious to rise at dawn, swim in the mountain stream, perform the familiar drill until he had out-performed everyone. He was more lean and disciplined than most. It was ironic to think how he had benefited from the seminary.

There was black smoke from a factory in the distance. They were his people working there. Tomorrow's hope. The death of Gyula and other emotional events had softened him for a while. It was a lesson. The chill words of Fust were the true reality. There was a world to be subdued and remade, and it would not crumble quickly. He would learn to move easily, like Fust, from the friendly word to the chill warning. There was a place for each. He would go back to the seminary prepared, steeled; they would not win him with softness. The history of the world showed that softness and love and humility were not worth a curse.

After drill, it was time for soccer, the freest thing he knew. He was not a great player. But most crucial was the will to win; it could overcome talent.

Soon, however, the young men surrounded him in a cluster; he saw in an instant it was prearranged.

"What's the deal, big shot?"

"What do you mean?"

"Why were you invited to the head table?"

"You a spy or something?"

The game was only three minutes old when the ball came to Hugo. One of them knocked him, which could have been accidental. Another ran over his leg. There was a crack and then pain up and down the body, pulsing. They carried him off. The doctor said it was broken. He said it would be fine later. He lay with his leg in a cast and suspended from the ceiling of a rustic room of the camp.

Two days later, as Hugo listened, forlorn, to the shouts of the drillmaster in the distance, the sound of a car intruded. Fust came through the door, brisk.

"Bad luck, my boy." There was no sympathy.

"Yes, sir."

"Broken, what?" He moved to the window, looked out at the mountains, keeping his distance.

"That's what the doctor said."

"If the doctor said it, it's probably true." Now Fust returned to look down on Hugo, a challenge in his voice. "It was an accident."

"Yes, sir."

Two weeks later, Hugo sat on the side of the same bed, gripping two crutches. A jolly doctor was examining his leg.

"If I may speak anatomically, son, that doctor didn't know his ass from a hole in the ground."

"What will happen?"

"Oh, you'll walk again. But that's because you're in such great shape — only a miracle would kill you."

"But these crutches...What'll happen to me?"

"I'm not God, son. There's no telling what might happen."

They let him go home a week before the others. Only a few said good-bye to him. The others eyed him suspiciously to the end. He had two secrets from them, tricky secrets to reconcile: he was a seminarian; and he had a special role in the Party. He hoped some day to find a friend he could tell.

Lies came easily to him. He had convincing stories for his parents about summer school. His brother too was home from camp, bitter, seldom at home. His parents were fearful and dispirited. The Party was taking a firmer grip on the country. His parents talked about it to Hugo but never in the presence of Ferenc — it would not be the first time that sons had turned on their parents.

"Couldn't we talk, Ferenc?" he said out by the wall on a Sunday when the parents were at Mass.

"You want me to go to confession?" Ferenc was sarcastic.

"No, and I don't want you to leave the Party, either."

Ferenc was taken aback but still suspicious. "If you think the Party is the answer, then you have to prove it to people, including your parents. Being mad at everyone won't prove anything."

"Do you know what they say about you at the meetings?"

"What?"

"What does it matter?" There was a gulf between them that might call for a bridge a mile long, or only an inch; it depended what the bridge was made of; it was impossible to know what was the right bridge.

"They don't understand, Ferenc."

Ferenc walked away. He too felt guilty about hurting their parents: Hugo could see it. But softening would do no good; kind words would not pacify them; they would want him back at Mass; they would want everything, no half-measures; there was no solution. The garden was overgrown with weeds. Their father was getting old and no longer seemed to care.

In early September, Hugo lurched on his crutches down the corridor to Ladislaus's room and knocked. The room inside was full of books and bric-a-brac. Ladislaus had his pipe in his mouth, blue smoke rising to the lamp in the ceiling. He untidily folded the newspaper he had been reading, threw it on the bed.

"Ah, Hugo? Come in and sit down."

"I won't be sitting." Hugo was flustered. "I came in to say I'm not suitable for all this."

"For what?"

"I can't go ahead, Father."

"Why don't you put down those damn crutches before you hurt somebody, most likely yourself." Hugo sat on a chair near the door, the crutches across his knees.

"Couldn't you throw me out — for being a cripple or something? Isn't that church law?"

"What's biting you, Hugo?" Ladislaus worked the dead pipe but with an attentive eye on his unhappy student.

"I'm scared."

"You of all people?"

"I'm not suitable. God damn it, Ladislaus, can't you see I'm not suitable?"

"Is there something you're not telling me?" Ladislaus looked searching at Hugo as if he knew clearly there was something else. Hugo returned the look for some moments. Then, as if courage had lost the battle, he rose and organized the crutches for departure. The air was full of ambiguity.

"I'll talk to you later."

Ladislaus rose, took a step after Hugo.

"Would you like a cup of tea?" Hugo did not turn, his face toward the door, just shook his head. "Men don't become priests because they're suitable — you know that, Hugo. We might think God is out of his mind when we see those he picks. Sure, he uses people like me to help him choose. Which proves he's out of his mind. Still, he gets by. And if you want to quit, don't expect me to do it for you."

There was a long silence. Hugo, without looking back at Ladislaus, opened the door and left.

Not long afterward, on a visiting Sunday, Hugo and Uncle Georg sat on the black iron chairs in the garden as the autumn leaves fell golden around them.

"They're bankrupt," Hugo said.

"I know," Fust replied.

Chapter Six

Hugo's limp dogged his climb to the altar. At twenty-six, he already had flecks of gray in his still-unruly hair. Five years had passed.

He took matches from his pocket to light the candles. As he lit the second candle, Jeno came stealthily from the sacristy and blew out the first. Hugo, unaware of Jeno's sabotage, returned to relight the first one as Jeno now put out the second.

"Stop that or I'll kick your butt."

They were practicing for Mass. Only a few weeks left to ordination. The lonely red sanctuary lamp hung from a rafter like a man from a cross.

"Ah, cheer up," Jeno said. "Jesus doesn't mind. Jesus is a card, like me." He climbed the altar steps in two bounds and tapped on the tabernacle door. "Hello, Jesus!" He waited, then turned to Hugo. "Sometimes he's not at home. He goes out to dinner at times. Especially when there are sourpusses around."

Jeno descended the steps in haughty disgruntlement, and Hugo followed.

"Introibo ad altare Dei."

"Ad Deum qui laetificat juventutem meam," Hugo responded. In the early years this was what he feared: approaching God on the altar, turning around and saying to all the expectant faces, "The Lord be with you." He had thought that eventually, some day, someone would stand up at the back and shout: I know about you. That fear was gone now. He had paid his dues; he was as qualified as Jeno, who made faces and tapped on Jesus' tabernacle door. The one great pity was the deception, felt especially at moments of closeness like this. There was an urge inside him to confide and tell. But he never could risk it, not even with Jeno.

Hugo walked beside Antal up the aisle of the old cathedral of Dunau-varos, dressed in the long white alb, the green stole across his back, the chasuble on his arm. Jeno was in front of him, serious now, no jokes or tricks. Miklos was farther in front. They were eleven in all. The people strained their necks for a look. He caught a glimpse of his mother, stooped and diminutive, eyes sternly ahead, having her own chat with God.

The smoke and smell of incense spread. The procession, with the bishop at the back, climbed the red-carpeted steps to the sanctu-ary and fanned out. White pillows were placed on the floor. The ordinandi prostrated themselves in front of the altar, heads on the pillows, as the universal church prayed a long prayer that God would be available today to come bearing the power in his mighty hand.

It was July 3, 1952.

"Ecce Sacerdos Magnus," the pent-up choir sang. The bishop wore his little green shoes and high miter, with acolytes dancing attendance. Not the God of the stable today, nor the God of the cross — there were different Gods for different occasions. Today it was the God of Pentecost, in flames of fire and dispensing gifts and courage and, Hugo hoped, a little clarity and, if one got really lucky, peace of mind.

The master of ceremonies clapped his discreet hands, and the or-dinandi arose from the pillows. There were readings from ancient scripture, and the Gregorian chant lifting the spirit so that, for the moment at least, Hugo was glad to be at the heart of all this. The bishop was not the star, nor even God: it was the ordinandi on whom all eyes were focused. God would never allow this memory to be spoiled for Hugo's mother — there had to be that much justice in the world. And if there were no God — either way, justice would somehow be done.

Ladislaus read their names to the hushed crowd after first chal-lenging: if anyone knows of a reason these young men should not go forward, let him speak. It was a formality of the ceremony, yet there was always the moment of suspense: someone might stand and know a reason and ruin the day. Or Fust might have one last trick to play. No one spoke, however, and after an eternity the ceremony moved forward amid ringing of bells.

The bishop rubbed oil on their hands. They went one by one to hold the chalice. He watched Jeno and thought of him once caressing that girl he gave up so blithely. He thought of the words of Fust resounding from six years ago — no marrying or women because we want our priest to be the best.

Jeno's head was up and his face absorbed; for him everything was making sense, the rubber mice and rubber turds all offered to God, who occasionally allowed moments of delirious joy. Hugo had felt it himself when he was young, such as after confession, and almost fell for it once or twice these last six years, moments of sheer un-alloyed happiness that no one ever even pretended existed except in the religious experience. If there was a God, let him give Hugo that dizzy joy now instead of this parched nothingness. Let God prove himself. Hugo would gladly tell Fust to go to hell for a little of that grace.

The bishop said the words of ordination, and in the blinking of an invisible eye they were all priests. Hugo searched for the face of Uncle Georg in the crowd but could not find him.

Afterward, in the sacristy, which had a floor of black flagstones, the bishop finally broke into a smile and shook their hands, then lined up with them for photographs. Soon he was gone.

"We did it, Hugo." Jeno came up next to him.

"We did."

"Congratulations, Hugo," Antal said, happy behind his thick glasses.

They went outside to meet their families and the happiness and the heartbreak. If a parent had died without seeing this day, it was heart-break. If a brother was a Communist and bitter, it was heartbreak. Days like this brought all of life into one big emotion, a time for re-membering and at the same time looking forward with hope or dread. It was impossible for humans to live just the moment and savor it.

His father and mother knelt, creaky and stiff, for his blessing, his mother kissing his hand according to custom and reluctant to let go. Others lined up, wanting to be blessed by the anointed hands. A special innocence and holiness were assumed to attach to the young priest, which somehow people suspected he would later lose.

In the afternoon, on the lawn, when his parents were not about, Fust approached him.

"Congratulations, Hugo."

"You had better kneel for a blessing, sir."

"Must I?"

"Down on your knees, Uncle Georg; there are people watching."

Fust went on his knees. Hugo blessed him solemnly, then held out his hands, and Uncle Georg had no option but to kiss them.

"You did it, boy." He was proud. Hugo's day was Fust's day too, years of planning reaching culmination.

"My parents will be coming back, sir."

"You may call me Zoltan now." He squeezed Hugo's hand and walked briskly to the big car, which lunged away. It was not the end of him. He was the other reality.

The light rain that fell in the mountains next morning did not deter the peasants who walked miles over rough roads to Hugo's first Mass. There were flags in the village and a band playing as he arrived in a car borrowed by the parish priest. When the rain cleared, the far mountains were purple and alive.

"Introibo ad altare Dei."

"Ad Deum qui laetificat juventutem meam."

He tried not to limp. Some in the congregation were young girls, and he realized amid vague loathing that he wanted to impress them. It was distressing that so useless a weakness was so close to the surface. When the girls came to the altar rails for Holy Communion, it was their pink tongues and soft lips he saw. And it was only white bread he saw himself placing on their tongues, not the God of the seminary and least of all the God of heaven.

His parents had the place of honor in the front row, the mother's eyes sparkling as they must have sparkled once on a night of courtship when it dawned on her that she was loved. There had been no Ferenc last night to greet the young priest, and none today.

Before the final blessing, the parish priest mounted the pulpit. He said in his thin voice that a great honor had been bestowed by God on the parish.

It became impossible to hear him because of the noise outside, shouting and drums beating, coming closer. The double doors at the back swung open and the intruders poured in. Their heavy boots clattered on the polished tiles, ten, twenty, perhaps thirty of them, lined up at the back, a few with guns. They stood silent. Hugo saw Ferenc among them, and he recognized other young men, their faces stony. The people eventually turned back to the priest.

"The harvest is ripe and we need more laborers," the thin voice said. "We need more young men like Father Ovath."

Hugo felt foolish sitting up there in his finery. The priest tapered his words to a quick finish. Hugo stood to give the blessing, holding his arms wide to embrace them all — that was the idea. Everyone knelt except the men at the back. "May the blessing of Almighty God, Father, Son, and Holy Spirit, descend on you and remain forever."

The young men were waiting at the gate afterward. "We can't let them get away with this," Hugo said. The least any spirited young priest would do was show indignation.

"Better not aggravate them, Father." The pastor seemed timid. How easily, it would seem, the church ought to fall to the Party. But by now Hugo knew better than anyone that something ran deep below the surface. He hated having this pastor call him Father — he should be slapping Hugo on the back and saying, "You son of a bitch, you made it," a comrade.

The entire village had planned to celebrate. With any luck, many of the men believed, they would be drunk by nightfall. But under this new threat of trouble, they just pushed forward to give their names and go home. At last there was only Hugo and the priest. He stopped in front of Ferenc.

"I have nothing to say to you," Ferenc said. And Hugo knew the gulf was so wide and their relationship so septic that only a miracle would restore the trust of their youth.

"What is your name?" the leader asked.

"You know my name," Hugo said. He was a former comrade from the mountain camp. Hugo could not remember his name.

"If you don't tell me, we will have to take you."

"My name is Hugo Ovath."

"That will be Father Ovath." He wrote it down, making Hugo the enemy.

Chapter Seven

"Say you'll come, Father."

"You don't need me, Lili."

"Now stop that, Father Hugo. The priest has always been the leader here."

He had been assigned to Berkos, a country parish. It had been a peasant community until the new regime undertook a program of industrialization and nationalization. The people's little farms and other properties were being taken away, and with these their independence and self-respect. They were angry and restless. There had been acts of sabotage followed by reprisals. There were confusion and dejection. There would be no hope without unity. That was why they were planning a protest meeting for Saturday night.

"Saturday nights I have confessions."

"After confession will do."

They had welcomed him ardently in August. The parish had been vacant for a year, so he carried on his back a daunting burden of hope. They cleaned the church, a small stone building, amid singing of old songs, and in the evening women brought cakes to the rectory. He inherited a housekeeper, Marta, who eyed him suspiciously and said little.

The parish hall was crowded on Saturday night. Villagers mingled with peasants from the country, everyone talking and joking. A thick cloud of smoke filled the room. Hugo, who did not smoke, sat among them. He enjoyed their rough humor, but he also felt obliged to study them; otherwise he would never be in a position to do what needed to be done to make them a part, one day, of the great future waiting to dawn. Some days that future was harder to envision than others, especially in a godforsaken place like Berkos, but if he didn't hold on to that hope there would be nothing, a gaping existential hole, or the psychological pit of despair.

"Up here, Father." Lili pointed to a chair at the head table beside herself. She was a strong dark girl with flashing teeth.

"I'm fine here — this isn't a church meeting."

"The priest is still the leader," she insisted. The others shouted no-nonsense agreement. "It will help to keep the peace," she explained. He let them see his limp as he walked up front. He was beginning to regard it as a badge of distinction. It hinted, at least in his own mind, at some past adventure that made him seem mysterious and maybe a hero. (Though one day not long after he'd arrived he had met a big man on the road outside Berkos with a limp just like his own. The big man eyed him with suspicion. It was too small a village for two limps like that.)

"Quiet, please, quiet I said." Lili was on her feet. They obeyed her with respect. "We all know why we're here. It would be easier — yes and safer too — to stay home, but here we are. The regime wants to take our land for development — that's it in a nutshell. And in some cases our houses. And our land and houses are all we've got — it's very simple really. We don't need another factory." She paused for attention. "We'll hear from Sandor first."

Sandor was a stocky man in his early sixties, his face eroded by work and weather. He wore three days' beard, had white wispy hair over big ears, and held a hat with a red feather in his hand. Hugo could soon see Sandor was a character. The others yelled their approval, and Sandor, with a droll grin, waved the old hat.

"Why are you picking on me?"

"Shut up, Sandor, and get on with it," Lili warned. Then Sandor turned serious, holding his hat on his chest and at times waving it for emphasis.

"You see what is happening elsewhere," he said. "They make promises. They tell us the land is still ours, and they're just managing it for us. Are we too stupid to manage it ourselves? Look what happened in Russia. And up north. The farmers were sent to the factories. You know as well as I do that the land is ours only until we hand it over to them."

When Sandor stopped the others murmured their approval.

"So we have to do something," he said.

"Talk is cheap, Sandor," one man said. "They always win."

"Only because we let them." Sandor was mad now. Water dripped in a corner of the hall. They were poor. The most valuable thing they had apart from themselves and each other was about to be taken away. It was one thing to read it in books, Hugo was thinking, Marx or Lenin or whoever, but this was more real than books, wives and children and self-respect and, on the other hand, the risk of getting hurt or killed.

"What the bloody hell can we do?"

"Oh, a thousand things," Sandor said. "We could go on strike. We could fight them if it came to that. But, before anyone panics — we could start with just a protest. Maybe a march."

"You can't leave it all to Sandor," Lili said.

"I say, fight them," a young man piped up, eyes fiery.

"Shut up!" an older man said.

"They can't send us all to labor camps," Sandor said. "That's why we must all stick together."

"What do you think, Father?" Lili asked.

He had known she would ask him. It was courtesy to ask the priest, but it was also a test of his mettle. Were he to speak words of fire, their hope would grow wings and soar. It would be the end of his career. But maybe the beginning of a different one. If he were prepared to limp ahead of them into battle, there was nothing they would not do. It would be another way into the history books: champion of the downtrodden, fighting for Sandor and the upstart young man who was told to shut up but also for his father and mother and a million like them. And if it went well there would be a statue one day where children would place flowers: here lies Hugo Ovath, who died for the people. Lili and all the others were looking at him.

"You must keep in mind that I have just arrived in Berkos, so I don't know all the facts."

"It's very simple, Father," Lili said. "They're going to take our land." Others murmured corroboration: that was all he needed to know.

"Peaceful protest is one thing, but you know the church's position on violence."

"Our land is ours, Father," one man shouted.

"And as for violence," Sandor spoke up. "The last priest we had here was Father Wortez. He stood up to them. I'm sure you heard what happened, Father. They said it was an accident, but everyone knows it wasn't an accident. He was a martyr."

"That's the truth; he was a martyr," another said. Hugo would soon be isolated.

"I just wanted to see how determined you were. My father is a peasant too, so I know how you feel." This brought a murmur of approval. "Yet it is your land and your families at stake. You must make the decisions, and you may rely on me to do what I can." This same group, he could see, would tell his successor with pride about how he willingly gave his life for their cause. Sacrifice was all they had.

After the meeting, they again milled about and talked.

"My father was killed the last time," Lili said, "along with Father Wortez."

"I'm sorry. You're very brave to be here."

Sandor approached, the cocky hat back on his head. "We're proud of you, Father Hugo. They'll leave us alone in the end. They can't kill us all, you know. Isn't Lili there the prettiest thing? I have my eye on her." He was already moving on, restless.

"And your wife has her eye on you, Sandor," Lili shouted after him. "Sandor is a poet," she explained to Hugo. "He used to write poems for the local paper until the Party took it over."

They seemed reluctant to go home. Community was life of a different kind than lonely individualism. They lived in each other, and then lived on in each other. This put life and even death in a more benign perspective.

The early sun was pushing its way through trees on the horizon as Hugo eased the old car out of Berkos and headed for the city forty miles away. After a mile he met the big man with a limp like his own, whose name was Daneel, occupying the middle of the road. Hugo slowed. Daneel would not move to the side. Hugo had to stop until he passed, glaring at the car and then at Hugo.

He drove as fast as the old car would go. The noisy vehicle was a gift from the Party by way of Uncle Georg. He explained to parishioners it was to bring the last rites to the dying. Years ago, Jesus could take his time on a donkey because he could raise the dead if he arrived too late.

First, there were people in the fields. They turned their heads to observe the passing car, giving themselves a break from stooping. Then there were factories, all new, steam seeping from pipes, with signs and directions, everything regulated, not free like the fields.

In the city, he drove cautiously through the streets. He was soon lost. He was reluctant to ask directions to Party headquarters, not wanting to attract attention in his black suit and plastic roman collar. Then in the distance he saw the domed building. A man in uniform told him where to park and watched him suspiciously limping up the stone steps.

"Zoltan Fust," he told an old wheezing man in a gray uniform behind a desk.

"What is your name?"

"It doesn't matter. Mr. Fust will see me."

"You would be surprised, sir, how many people say that. I must have your name." He coughed, then dragged on a cigarette and put it flat on the desk where other cigarettes had burned a pattern of black lines and blotches in the wood. He did not like priests, Hugo could sense it. Then he asked himself if he was getting too sensitive. The mind playing tricks. The problem was to know when the paranoia was real.

"Ovath is my name."

"Your first name?"

"Hugo. Look — just tell Mr. Fust I'm here."

"Does that plastic collar irritate you?"

Hugo looked steadily at the old man. Perhaps it was an honest question from an eccentric old man. "No, you can't see Mr. Fust," the eccentric old man said.

"I don't like your attitude, sir." Hugo felt he had given paranoia its due. "I'll have you reported."

"My apologies, sir. Of course you may wait, if you wish, but Mr. Fust won't be back until tomorrow."

Hugo scrawled a note for Fust, suggesting Sandor be removed for a while — he could be troublesome. Indeed, he was troublesome already, causing Hugo to be insulted by this broken old man. He was unhappy about leaving a note. He and Fust needed to work out some system. In the church he had devoted six years to preparing for every eventuality, while the Communists operated by the seat of their Communist pants. The church, of course, had much more practice, having centuries of a head start.

He spent the day exploring the city, alone and uneasy. Driving home in the dark, he passed Sandor's house. There was a light in the window, a picture of peace, but Sandor was probably inside hatching plans and further trouble. A poet, that was his problem.

Chapter Eight

"Introibo ad altare Dei."

He offered Mass every morning, attended only by a few elderly women, each an island of overcoats and woolen scarves scattered among the pews. They came up afterward to light candles, hoping for wonders. Hope would have grabbed Hugo too if he allowed it. There were other things he would reach for first if he got lucky and found them at the end of some rainbow: wealth or an end to his limp or a willing girl, things he could more reliably count on. But if none of these came up, it was a temptation to pilfer hope. It might carry him through tomorrow and then the day after; and even if at the end it turned out to be emptiness and nothingness, he need not care — he would be dead.

"Ad Deum qui laetificat juventutem meam," the altar boy answered.

Conventional wisdom said that after a while the Mass would become mechanical, no big deal, but he could never get through it without some thought intruding — What if, what if? It proved nothing either way that the prayers never seemed to be answered. It would be unreasonable to expect a God with a lot on his mind to push buttons for specific prayers. If wealth or health came, it was chance. If a girl materialized, it was chance. And materialize she sometimes did, in the city, in Berkos, in the fields, throwing a glance and then looking away, saying something enigmatic and then taking it back in the next instant. If he grabbed the chance, it might be happiness. But it would also be a sin, a sin against the Party, which was less forgiving than God.

It was the same each morning: an endless cycle of possibilities and distractions. It would always be like that. It was easy for Jeno, Hugo thought: no doubts to cope with; or for Miklos; or for the old man who stopped him one day on the road.

"God is good, Father." He was a big man with a round chest. He was poor. Hugo figured it would not be hard to make him happy.

"Good news, then?"

"Bad news, Father. My wife is dead. Could you come and see her?"

He did not, at that moment, want to go and see a dead woman. He remembered the dark priest in the mountains who always climbed the winter hills on his bicycle to share their sorrows. He remembered his promise to Fust to be the best priest in the country.

"Jump in," he said. The old man was nervous in the car, holding on to the seat with his bony hands. There was no one at the house, only a scrawny dog barking. He had wild flowers in a glass jar beside the bed.

"Was it sudden?"

"Twenty years, Father." She had not been out of the bed for twenty years. "But it's all right now; she's happy now." And then he cried, his big chest heaving. He never gave up in twenty years of lifting and feeding her. The neighbors stopped calling, he said, because she used to lose her head and shout obscenities at them.

"Any children?"

"None, father." He was as alone as Hugo, and he said God was good. Perspective was everything. At the funeral Mass he willed that she would be out there somewhere waiting for him and no longer crazy, shouting obscenities.

The altar boy poured water and wine, and Hugo washed the chalice. There was a musty smell of dampness. Churches needed crowds to be successful. Yet churches of all stripes were among the least-used edifices on earth. After he removed his vestments, he knelt as if to pray; he skipped no ritual even when no one was watching — it was what the best priest on earth would do. He was interrupted by the heavy boots of a youth running through the church.

"Come quickly, Father — it's murder."

He wasted no time. He retrieved the oils from a little locked box in the sanctuary. The boy was waiting at the car for a ride.

"Who?"

"Sandor."

"Where?" He knew the answers. The questions were a formality.

"At his house, Father. I'll show you."

A small crowd had gathered in front of the house. Sandor was lying under a tree, still alive. There was blood on the roots of the tree, on the grass, seeping through Sandor's shirt. His head lolled back. Hugo wished Sandor had died immediately.

"Why didn't you take him inside?"

"He wouldn't let us."

"Did you send for a doctor?"

"He didn't want that either."

His wife knelt beside him, moaning softly, caressing his face. Hugo too knelt and leaned close to Sandor. "Sandor, can you hear me?"

"They got me, Father." The words were low.

"We'll take you inside," Hugo said. They had splattered him with bullets, some wounds bleeding, others already dried up and gaping.

"No, it's more comfortable here. Confession, Father."

The wife moved away, and the other neighbors followed suit, their faces in shock. Anger and hatred would settle in later, but without Sandor to drive them their rebellion would dissipate. Sandor was the one. Yet there was no need to kill him, Hugo thought, his own hate rising.

"How long, Sandor?" he said in Sandor's ear.

"Only a few weeks. And all the usual sins, Father. I confessed them already. Had no time for sin since my last confession." He was getting weaker. It was amazing he was still alive, an iron man from the mountains. He had inner resources wrested from the earth and the air and the sky, a lifetime of squinting at life and taking its measure — go ahead, ask him before it's too late.

"You know, Sandor, that God forgives those who forgive. Before giving you absolution, I want you to forgive those who did it."

For the first time he turned his eyes on Hugo, not clear like at the meeting but glazed and bloodshot.

"I'm happy now, Father, that you're here."

"Say you'll forgive," Hugo whispered desperately. But Sandor's head dropped ever so slightly. He would never say the words of forgiveness.

His wife came back. She knew he was dead. Hugo gave Sandor's departing spirit absolution. Theologians said the soul lived on, hung around for an hour or two, reluctant to leave the body it knew so well. "Deinde te absolvo a peccatis tuis." Hugo saw or imagined he saw that shining part of Sandor, the immortal part, waving its hat with a red feather in it.

"Do you know who did it?" he asked those gathered around.

"Two men, Father."

"Who saw?"

They looked down at Sandor's wife, still holding the body, her round face streaked with tears and blood on her hands. What did it matter who did it?

"Help her take the body inside."

But she turned on Hugo. "He said you would carry on the fight, Father. Just before you arrived. He knew he was dying. He said you would lead us."

They placed Sandor on the wrinkled sheets of the big bed, and someone took off his heavy boots. They knelt down and Hugo led them in prayer, the Joyful Mysteries. Sandor's wife did not answer the prayers at first, then picked them up in a whisper, and before the rosary was over she had drawn courage from somewhere — "Pray for us sinners, now and at the hour of our death."

"We must do something," a man with a wiry beard like horsehair said. "We must revenge Sandor."

"Revenge won't bring Sandor back."

"We can't sit and do nothing." Now several men had joined them.

"That's different. We have a right to defend ourselves." Hugo began to see an opportunity.

This time it was easy to find the big building with the dome. Fust came round from behind his big desk to greet Hugo, expansive.

"There was no need to kill him," Hugo said.

"Don't worry about that, Hugo. Sandor — that old geezer could have caused us interminable trouble."

"What the hell do you know about him? He was harmless, I tell you." Hugo owed it to Sandor to be angry. He owed it to his own integrity.

"Now listen to me." Fust slapped the desk, no longer affable. "We had our plans made before we ever heard from you. You merely corroborated our view, nothing more. This may be a relief to you if you're feeling squeamish about what happened. But don't dare come in here dictating to us. Do you understand me?" He paced the office, poised between good and bad humor.

"You know everything — you and God."

"I wouldn't be too sure about God."

"You must tell me what to do," Hugo said, softening. There was a time to be conciliatory, and this was surely it.

"You'll learn," Fust said. "And we really are grateful for what you did." He could move from sweet to sour with great ease, from life to death.

"There's going to be further trouble."

"No, not without Sandor."

"They are looking to me for leadership. I have a suggestion." So they talked for hours. Hugo was learning from Fust how to be pliable, how to move from mood to mood. They went downstairs to eat in the big Party cafeteria. In the end Fust was enthusiastic. He would cooperate; Hugo had his word.

Afterward, they talked about soccer. Fust spoke at length of his family. He had a boy ten years old who was delicate. It hurt him that this boy acted like a girl and was bullied by other boys at school. He was reluctant to let Hugo go until late into the night. Hugo was beginning to understand: it was a night on which Fust gave himself permission to be vulnerable and wear his heart on his sleeve.

They came from every direction for Sandor's funeral. They came on foot or on bicycles or with horse and wagon. Each trek was an act of defiance against the regime. They were angry. They knew much was at stake, their futures. A few careless words could turn them to violence.

Hugo spoke from the altar, reminded them about forgiveness and patience. They listened sullenly and patiently. This was Sandor's day. They would send him off with dignity.

"We will have the demonstration Sandor wanted," Hugo said at the graveside, Sandor's wife by his side. "On Saturday morning. We will fight for our rights."

They knelt in the fresh clay and prayed for the soul of Sandor, already a prophet and making miracles happen from the other side.

"You should stay out of it," the housekeeper said on Friday evening.

"Why, Marta?"

"It will be like Father Wortez. Everyone knows they did it." She left the room. It was not a conversation but a warning.

On Saturday morning the little roads were filled with people. They milled about the village street, talking and excited, no shape to the crowd, waiting for someone to give them direction. The dark-haired Lili walked among them, talking to men who might grow into leaders. But she too was waiting for Hugo.

He emerged at ten from the rectory, came limping down the middle of the street. They clapped and cheered as he drew closer, congregating around him.

"You must tell them what to do, Father," Lili said, giving him all the opportunity he needed.

"They must be disciplined and orderly." They shuffled about in a vain effort to be orderly. "We'll march to Party headquarters." Two representatives of the Party worked in a wooden hut at the bottom of the village. It was never clear what work they did, but they were the eyes of the Party in the village.

Hugo moved out into the street, and the leaders lined up beside him — Sandor's wife, the man with the wiry beard, and others. There were posters with the usual slogans bobbing in the crowd, a bit superfluous, Hugo thought, no one to see them since the whole village was in the procession.

Outside the Party hut they shuffled to a stop. When the song they were singing was finished, there was a silence. Lili stepped forward.

"Thank you for coming out. It was the right thing to do, and you won't regret it. Father Hugo will now speak."

A small flurry of applause followed. Hugo stood on a boulder by the roadside and gazed out at the villagers, their faces intent, squinting into the sun. He knew what was at stake. All their hopes were pinned on his promise to fight for them and the implied promise to die if necessary. He realized for the first time that was what counted: what you were prepared to die for. They would be looking for that in him. Never having won the great victory, they knew from experience that sacrifice was the most they could hope for. Sacrifice gave life meaning. It meant some things were more important than others, worth living and striving for.

"We are all here except one — Sandor," he began. "But our being here is proof that Sandor did not die for nothing." He had rehearsed it well, anticipated what they wanted to hear, incorporated what he knew he could deliver. Not having Sandor's fire to raise their spirits, his ace in the hole was to deliver what he promised. He had a letter in his pocket, he said, a letter he would deliver on their behalf to the Party representatives in the hut, serving notice that he would lead the people in strikes and disruptions until the Party withdrew its intention to nationalize their property.

"I promise you that no one will take your land from you, that we will stand united until the new regime realizes it must listen to the voice of the people. I will now submit this letter in your name."

The noise that came back was at first a deep drone rising to a whine as gray trucks came over the hill, five, six, seven, the wide crates lined with soldiers looking out from every side, the secret police. They surrounded the crowd in a sweeping circle. The tailgates dropped with a clatter, and the soldiers jumped out with their guns ready and bayonets attached, dark sinister blades. An officer shouted through a megaphone: "illegal gathering . . . disrespect for the law . . . disperse or take the consequences."

There was a short stunned moment, followed by shouts of anger and cries of panic, flailing and shoving and people falling to the ground. Above this pandemonium was heard one sharp crack of a rifle, causing a momentary pause in the shouting and anger.

From his position by the wall, Hugo saw a man go down. A soldier stood over him, gun at the ready. Hugo leaped from the wall, and in a few giant strides was on the scene, punching the soldier, who fell on top of the fallen protester. "You murderer," Hugo shouted.

The soldier got up slowly and deliberately, not taking his eyes from Hugo. Before he could shoot, another soldier knocked Hugo to the ground with a lunge. The crowd had moved back. They could see Hugo on the ground, dirty, nose bloody.

Nothing ever went according to plan, Hugo thought in the split seconds he waited there for possible death. He realized at that incongruous moment that some of his best thoughts came to him at times like this when there was no time for thinking. Something more had to happen before he died, he now realized. This was no way to round out a life, even if Fust, for all he knew, had decreed it. Some purpose had to be accomplished first. There was nothing yet, only a beginning.

"Somebody help that man," Hugo shouted. A protester rushed forward to the wounded man. With his bayonet the first soldier prodded Hugo to his feet. An officer emerged from the back of another truck and sauntered forward.

"Take him," the officer said.

Before he was led off, Hugo turned to the protesters. "Go home quietly. You have my promise nothing will happen to you, and no one will take what is yours." He was hustled into a truck. He made no effort to stanch his bloody nose. I'm a sight they'll remember no matter what happens, he thought as he looked back at them. Bravado was mixed with fear in his tumbling thoughts. If these security soldiers killed him — if he were to be double-crossed by Fust — he would live on in many memories until the day the last of these Berkos people died.

At the police station, a dozen soldiers were fighting a losing battle with boredom, playing cards, chatting and laughing too loudly as they drank cheap beer. From a back room an officer came forward and sat opposite Hugo.

"Look at us, Father," he said. "There are more of us than there are things to do. That's bad news for someone in your position." He was an aristocratic type with an ironic demeanor, swishing a cane in an extravagant way. "You accosted a member of the security police."

"He shot a man. . . ."

"Save it, save it. You want a smoke before we kill you?" Now he had the total attention of the other soldiers. Killing always got people's attention, no matter which side of it one was on.

"I want to talk to Zoltan Fust."

"You're a funny fellow, Father."

"In the presence of these soldiers I am warning you that you will have to answer for it if you do not contact Mr. Fust." It was the only card Hugo had, and this seemed a good time to play it. If it failed, he would be dead. But the officer seemed to hold the view that he would be dead anyway.

"Put him in number four."

It was a miserable, dank cell. There was a blanket on the floor, and when the cold became unbearable, he put the blanket round his shoulders. He promised himself that if he survived this he would start keeping a diary. The prison experience — What did people know about it? The utter loneliness in the quiet of the night. The insects, and bigger vermin, rats. And the fear of whatever might happen next. Some day it might be important to let people know what he had been through.

Then he heard the door unlocking. He guessed it was the small hours of the morning; he must have dropped off to sleep in his misery. The officer came in and closed the door behind him.

"Why did you do that, Father?"

"What?"

"Mr. Fust doesn't know you. Does that surprise you?"

"No." It didn't matter what answer he gave. The officer spoke softly. Hugo preferred people who were loud and blustery.

"You had me scared there for a while," the officer said. "But not anymore. You are to die at dawn." He turned and left. Hugo looked up at the pitch darkness for the sign of a window that later might tell him when dawn was approaching, but he could see nothing in the blackness. It was a devilish time for crowding thoughts. How could he be the best priest on earth if he kept getting into scrapes like this? Or perhaps Fust had concluded that the best priest on earth was a dead one.

He was awakened again by someone at the door. Two soldiers entered. A little window high in the wall was letting in the dread light of day. One soldier produced a blindfold.

"I don't need that," Hugo said grandly. He feared he would panic as soon as he was fully awake.

"You don't have a choice, comrade."

They took him outside to a courtyard. The blindfold created confusion and the beginning of panic. He couldn't tell whether someone was holding a gun to his head. Then the soldiers grabbed him and threw him into a truck. It was a beautiful bruised feeling: he was still alive.

"I demand to see an officer," he shouted. Nobody bothered to respond, not even to mock him. This was bad news. The truck droned and lurched forward. Long before journey's end the world unaccountably tilted his way again: he could feel his spirits rising because deep inside something told him they were taking him home. They pushed him off the truck, and he fell in a heap with another beautiful thud. The truck drove away groaning as he lay motionless until the sound had faded. He cautiously removed the blindfold. He guessed it was nearly noon. There was no one in sight. Berkos was like a ghost town.

He knocked on his own front door. There was no response. He went from window to window, knocking and shouting progressively louder. The back door was open. Marta would never allow that.

"Marta!"

The door of her room was ajar. A large brass clock still ticked on the table. A suitcase was on the bed, some of her clothes in it, the rest on the floor. She had been about to leave, before something happened that changed her plans. Old predictable Marta pulling a surprise of her own.

"Dominus vobiscum." When he turned around from the altar next morning there was no one there, so he had to respond to himself, "et cum spiritu tuo."

A letter arrived. "Congratulations, my boy. And welcome home. But please be advised that I am not acquainted with country clerics. Yours. Uncle Georg."

Hugo hated him briefly. For Fust it was a game. An experiment. Fust had little to lose either way, least of all his life.

A big black car arrived the next day, cruised slowly through the village, filling the narrow street, driven by a chauffeur. It stopped at Solti's shop, a purple building where you could buy groceries or clothes or equipment for the farm.

"We're looking for the priest named Ovath." The man from the car had a handlebar mustache and looked important in a splendid suit.

"You won't find him here," Solti said. Although Solti was a Communist, the people still liked him because he told jokes, but especially because he gave them credit and never put the squeeze on them. It was said he was a sailor on a Russian ship when he was young and saw the revolution in Moscow and was a supporter ever since, though Solti himself never talked about it.

"This is a small village; you might know where he is," the important man suggested.

"Probably out visiting the sick."

Outside the village, a man stopped Hugo, waving frantically. "They're waiting for you, Father."

"Who?"

"It must be the Party. Two men in a big car. You should hide until they're gone."

Hugo walked up the village street until the man from the car stopped him.

"Is your name Ovath?"

"Yes."

"We have a letter for you." The car drove away without a further word from anyone. Hugo walked home, two stray dogs following him, knowing he was being watched with great interest from every window.

For the rest of the week he strode from door to door, a man on a mission. His suit was still dirty from his joust with the army. We will march again on Saturday, he said at every door. We mustn't give up now. Don't be afraid. But they were afraid. They promised to be there on Saturday, but he could see their wills bending before the enormous unseen pressure of the Party.

Instead of the thousands of a week ago, there were a few ragged dozen. Lili took her place beside him. She flashed her white teeth in a warm smile when he shook her hand and gave it an added squeeze of encouragement. The band was a skeleton of its former self. They shuffled along, no placards, no singing.

When they reached the hut that was Party headquarters, the little procession stopped. This time, Lili did not bother to introduce Hugo, who stood on the same boulder as before and gazed out over his little flock in a dramatic silence until eventually they grew uncomfortable.

"I'm sorry the numbers are so small," he began. "I know it's not easy. And I know things happen. But, on the other hand, sometimes risks have to be taken. Where is the people's faith? What happened to the belief that the future can be better than the past?" He paused and took a letter from his pocket and opened it slowly. "I have here a letter from the Department of the Interior. It says that, due to the special circumstances, the Party has decided to leave untouched the land and property of this parish."

He stopped and folded the letter as deliberately as he had opened it. Their good fortune gradually dawned on his listeners. They cheered and laughed and then ran from house to house down the village street spreading the good news. Lili threw her arms around Hugo's neck and gave him a hearty kiss on the cheek before running off to her own family. In the end Hugo was left to walk home alone. He couldn't decide who had won a victory. Perhaps everyone.

Hours later, he sat in his small study as the shouting and revelry came faintly from the village street. On the wall was a print of Raphael's Sistine Madonna and a photograph of ordination day, Ladislaus and the bishop in the middle. In the houses of old priests there was always such a picture on the wall, turned brown and faded, the priest's family and destiny.

He began his new diary: "Only a beginning has been made. There will be many a broken heart, many a stab of pain, many a cry of betrayal before people realize that the old ways are gone and that they are flame of the new fire, and then somewhere down the long road the charred world will become cities of gold and countryside of green and laughing people waving."

Chapter Nine

Twelve priests of various ages, dressed in their clerical suits, trickled into the big dining room of what used to be the bishop's house. They were garrulous and joking, putting a brave face on life, happy in one another's company.

The room had been ransacked. Furniture was broken. A picture of the pope, Pius XII, stripped of its frame, leaned askew on the mantelpiece. One priest was lighting a wood fire. Antal was lining up unmatched chairs by the long dusty oak table.

Hugo came through the door, and they broke into spontaneous, raucous applause, hooting and joking and slapping him on the back.

"Here he is, by God, the hero of Berkos!"

"Tell us about it, Ovath."

"Nothing to tell." Hugo waved them away.

Jeno came through the door and was greeted with a wide range of incoherent and jokey noises. Popular Jeno.

Finally the monsignor arrived, an old, fragile man, shaking hands with everyone and apologizing for everything.

"Sorry I'm late, lads. Sorry, now, sorry. Punctuality is the politeness of kings. Louis XIV said that, you know, or was it Louis XV?" He had the reputation of being a saint, but he was inefficient and always late.

Meanwhile, Hugo and Jeno engaged in their usual bear hug.

"You're a stranger," Hugo said. "I never see you anymore."

"You know where I live," Jeno said, too solemnly.

The monsignor arrived with his hand out.

"Hello, Jeno."

"I'm Hugo, Monsignor. This one here is Jeno."

"Hugo is the ugly one, Monsignor. I'm the other one."

"I have been reading your publications, Hugo. Very good, very good."

"His cartoons are the best, in my opinion," Jeno added.

Hugo had to guide the monsignor to the top of the table, then held the chair for him. The old man searched aimlessly through his briefcase.

"There's nothing but trouble," he began. "They're out to get us. If they don't allow us to raise money for the seminary, we'll have to close down."

"Any word about a new bishop?" Miklos asked.

"They won't budge on that either. They never say no, but it's obvious they have no intention."

"They budge sometimes," a priest said. "They're very practical and will give way to the right pressures."

"Yeah, look at Ovath," Antal said. "They gave in to Hugo."

"Yes, indeed," the monsignor agreed. "A miracle, if you ask me."

"One thing I learned," Hugo said. "They will not give in to defiance. It helps to let them see that the church can be reasonable."

"Perhaps Hugo is right," the monsignor agreed, still shuffling papers, searching for something. "Perhaps some of them are reasonable."

"It's no use," Jeno exploded. "We can not compromise with them and that's that. They killed that old man, Sandor. And thousands of others. We have to oppose them; we have to make a moral statement."

"Jeno is right," a priest said.

"I agree," another said.

"I disagree," Antal said. "Opposing them like that will merely give them an excuse to put us all away."

"They're already putting us away," Jeno shouted louder. "They will keep pushing us back until we stop and fight."

"We can be united and strong without fighting," Hugo said more quietly.

"I'm disappointed in you, Hugo." Jeno was angry.

"Who the hell cares?" Hugo was angry too.

"Boys — stop bickering this minute," the monsignor admonished them. "We have practical matters to deal with."

The meeting droned on for two hours. When it was over Jeno came across the room and put a mock stranglehold on Hugo.

"You never could listen to reason."

"You never had any," Hugo replied.

"You never come to visit me anymore."

"You never stay home long enough." Memory was a killer. He

remembered the September day when Jeno volunteered to carry his suitcase because, he said, people should carry one another's burdens. It was an impossible mandate. Each had to carry his own.

Most of the priests were reluctant to go home. Three were in a corner sharing a story; they knew more dirty jokes than the young men at summer camp. As Jeno used to say, it was no harm to discuss the menu so long as you didn't touch the food.

"You must send me all your publications," the monsignor said. "And you must continue to write. We need scholarship to fight the enemy in these changing times." The monsignor was said to be translating the *Iliad* into verse.

Chapter Ten

Driving home on a pitch dark night, Hugo saw ahead of him the big, scowling, limping man who seemed to haunt the roads. He wouldn't budge. Hugo stopped, got out of the car.

"Is that a genuine limp or are you making a mockery of me?" the big man asked. "You're a goddamn, shit-faced bitch's son of a priest."

"Whoa! What's the matter with you?"

"Shit-ridden son of a bitch — may your next stop be in hell."

"Son of a bitch yourself." Hugo decided to take a more aggressive approach to the fellow. "Get your fucking carcass off the fucking road or I'll break your fucking neck."

The big farmer looked fiercely at Hugo for a long time, and a half-smile gradually broke across his face. "Damn, I can talk to you," he said, "because I can see you're damned like myself."

On a beautiful day Jeno was rowing lazily as Hugo reclined in the stern of a blue boat on a lovely lake beneath the mountains. Swans swam nearby. A sunny island beckoned.

"'Get your carcass off the fucking road or I'll break your fucking neck,' I said to him."

"Son of a bitch." Jeno was impressed.

"It turns out, he killed a man during the war. He was left alone with this prisoner who called him names for two days, so my man drowned him in a stream, held him under the water."

"Good God."

"Can't get it out of his mind since. He thinks he's damned. But he decided to go to confession anyway, since he thinks I'm damned too. Misery loves company, he said."

"He's right about that — you being damned and all." Jeno's rubber face grinned like it did in the old days. It was amazing to Hugo how often people unwittingly came so close to the truth. And if there was any truth at all, it was that Hugo was damned. So often in the past he thought of spilling the beans to Jeno. Risking it all. Let whatever was to happen happen — that was how close Hugo had come to his own ruination. Only now could he see the unyielding steel core of Jeno, stainless steel that couldn't be dented. And yet, on that lovely lake, each could truthfully say that they had no better friend on earth. Being damned was complicated.

"Welcome, Monsignor."

"Sorry I'm late, Hugo." He was an hour late. The letter had been cryptic: he wanted to discuss an important matter. Hugo was sure the monsignor could no longer distinguish which matters were important.

They talked about Marta the housekeeper, disappeared a year ago. Even Fust had made inquiries; there was no record anywhere.

"I'm sorry, Monsignor — afraid the roast is badly burned." He came from the kitchen with a platter of charred meat.

"Your book, Hugo — I knew there was something I wanted to thank you for. A great book, a great book."

"Thanks, Monsignor." It had been published two months earlier. Titled *On Earth as It Is in Heaven*, it had been favorably reviewed in important magazines, groundwork for a new theology for the changing times. Hugo had carefully held on to all the icons of the past, but reminded readers that the whole known world was no longer Christian, which of course it never was except in some ecclesiastical minds. And reminding readers too that, like it or not, one of the new forces on the world scene was Communism. He made no case for it, but by repeated mention he hoped to attune minds to acceptance of it, making it seem reasonable and practically part of the accepted world order, which of course was imperfect but could be improved. If the monsignor said no more about it, that meant he had not read the book.

"Some of it seems a little at odds with traditional teaching, if you ask my opinion. For example, our belief that the Kingdom has already begun."

"Just a matter of emphasis is all."

"Which brings me to the point." The monsignor put down his wine glass and cleared his throat. "We need another man at the seminary. All the fingers are pointing at you."

"But Monsignor." Hugo, despite all his scheming, was genuinely surprised. "I have no degrees." Those destined to teach in the seminary spent years getting degrees in Rome or Louvain or even America. New possibilities opened up, of years abroad, later on, to get those degrees, travel, and learn foreign languages, free, for a while, from his double life, a chance to study how the rest of the world lived, and, hell, a chance to stay away and never come back if he found some secret of happiness abroad that was missing here at home.

"I know, I know, but our backs are to the wall, Hugo. I'll be perfectly frank with you: what we need right now, more than erudition, is someone who can negotiate with the regime. We're on the brink of financial collapse."

"We need a bishop, Monsignor."

"Yes, of course." The old man got mad as hell. "They're exasperating, those people. Sometimes I think Jeno is right — that there is no way but to stand up and fight them toe to toe." Then he subsided, perhaps slightly embarrassed at the picture he had suggested of himself fighting anyone toe to toe. "Ladislaus is no diplomat. But you have had considerable success in that direction, Hugo."

The monsignor left in the dark, but forgot to turn on the lights until his car was out of the village.

"Is that Uncle Georg?" The voice on the phone assured him it was. "Your nephew needs to talk to you."

Hugo was beginning to feel at home at Party headquarters. He now had a lofty excuse for being there if anybody got inquisitive: he was the church diplomat wrangling with the regime for concessions.

The wheezy old man had been replaced at the front desk by a young woman in her twenties. The Party had painted the vestibule and added a portrait of Lenin and was obviously upgrading the place. Eva was the final touch of class. She had two prominent ivory teeth, long auburn hair, and a friendly, slightly mocking attitude. It was all designed, Hugo guessed, to make headquarters more human and less forbidding. Hugo approved. Especially of Eva.

"Ovath, isn't it?"

"How did you know?"

"Mr. Fust will be ready in a minute." He was about to take a seat.

"And Mr. Ovath?"

"Yes?"

"Don't be surprised. We know everything here." This left Hugo uncertain whether she was joking or whether indeed she knew, as she said, everything.

"What's your name?"

"Eva. You must be important, coming here to see himself."

"And you must be important — sitting there and keeping people away from himself." As this wobbly conversation got out of control Hugo realized he was smitten. He would sell his soul that very minute to have this woman for his own. And although he knew little about women, he had the giddy feeling that she was feeling a somewhat similar turbulence. Each was looking at the other in desperate need of a reason to keep the conversation going.

"What is it like?"

"What do you mean?"

"You know — being a priest?"

But the phone rang. It was Fust. Hugo promised to tell her about priests some other time.

"I'm finished here at five. You could tell me then."

"One thing I can tell you right now about a priest: he is not supposed to appear in public with beautiful women."

"So — you can come to my house."

"That's even worse." He climbed the stairs looking over his shoulder. "Can't keep the man waiting." He needed to get away from her before he lost his head.

Fust was all business, so Hugo got to the point immediately: "They want me to teach at the seminary."

"It's not what we had hoped, is it?"

"I can't really refuse."

"It was that book. The damn thing was too successful."

"Have you read it?"

"I know nothing about theology. I glanced at it. It seemed fine." There was a photo of a boy on his desk, the delicate son by whom he was troubled and embarrassed. He seemed about ten. He seemed so innocent.

"They expect me to get money for the seminary. That's their primary agenda."

"What do you think of that?"

"I think it might be a good idea. You might even consider a government subsidy."

"Why in hell would we do that?"

"Because it would give you power over them. The power to pull the plug and put them out of business."

"You're a smart priest. I'll think about it. Now get out of here."

Hugo had a great desire to pick up the huge desk and throw it out the window where it would keep on spinning into orbit, Fust's damned papers flying in all directions, the little boy's photo shining in the sun, but all the rest ending on a garbage dump in hell. Fust held all the power; that was the problem. When Fust said get out, it was time to get out. There were young Fusts everywhere, who could do the job just as well as this crabby man, but there was only one Hugo, a prize, and unappreciated by this bastard who of all people ought to know better. Oh yes, he would throw Fust out the window after the desk.

He descended the big stairway in a rage.

"Good-bye, Mr. Ovath," she said.

"What did you say your name was?"

"Eva."

"Eva — would you join me for dinner?"

"Well, this is a surprise. I thought priests couldn't eat with females. Or have the rules changed?"

"We'll make an exception."

Eva knew the kind of place: a dark little restaurant on a side street where people talked quietly and the waiter brought the bottle of wine for inspection before opening it.

Across a nearby table a young couple held hands.

"So what is it like — being a priest?"

"No, you tell me: What is it like to work for the Party?"

"It's just a job."

"Just a job? I thought Party members lived for the cause, like being a priest."

"Some do. Fust, for example."

"But not you?"

"Not me." It seemed surprising frankness considering that they had just met. That meant she had nothing to fear from anyone. She was who she was, Eva, who worked for Fust, who could presumably fire her, but ultimately she was not crucial enough in anybody's plan that she need worry about a thing.

He feasted his eyes on her, hoping this devouring concupiscence wasn't too obvious. She had applied more makeup than at work. I want to see her as she really is, he thought, without the cover-up.

He told her about the people of Berkos. He praised the Party for letting them keep their land. Sure, he was clapping himself on the back, but she seemed eager to see him as a hero and egged him on until, tongue loosened by the wine, he told her of his likely transfer to the seminary.

"Congratulations!"

"Not yet. It still depends on you-know-who."

"You're an odd couple — you and you-know-who."

"Like you and me." His guard had gone up. She could be speaking out of curiosity or because she liked him, or it could be a trap. "Every couple is odd until you figure out how they were thrown together and what factors moved them to be a couple in the first place. It's usually something ordinary and boring." He knew how to dance around tricky subjects, but especially this one.

"I hope we can do this again," she said at the end.

"I'm not so sure it's a good idea."

"At my place perhaps?" He was amazed at how direct she was. All his training warned him that women were coy and even duplicitous and what you saw was not what you were likely ultimately to get. "What's wrong with being an odd couple?"

"We'll see."

He played it cautiously, but he drove home on a cloud of romantic anticipation. Crooked life might yet have a turn or two left.

Chapter Eleven

In September he carried his cases down the long seminary corridor at Dunauvaros. He stopped in front of the picture of the dead Bishop Illyes. They were tied together for life; it was useless to turn his head and try not to look. Illyes was such a well-kept secret, so seldom mentioned; it was strange.

"Good to see you, Hugo," Ladislaus was at the top of the stairs, arms flailing.

"Good to see you, Ladislaus."

He led the way to the room where Gyula died. There would be one friendly ghost. The room was as bare as when Hugo was a student. Christ still hung from the rough cross on the wall. There was the same smell of floor wax. And outside, the birds still sang in the beautiful garden, perfectly tended as if no weeds had grown, no seasons come or gone, since the first day he arrived and stupid Jeno had suggested that they carry each other's load.

"I hope you're glad to be back, Hugo."

"I'll tell you at the end of the year. I bet you had something to do with this."

"Well, if you insist, I did mention your name. And to be totally honest, I'm hoping you can do something about the finances. You're coming aboard a sinking ship, you know. And you seem to have a way of getting concessions from the regime."

They went down to the refectory where four priests were drinking coffee and smoking interminably.

"Do you play poker, Hugo?" one asked. "We need a fourth."

"Not very well, but I'll give it a try."

"It seems, Hugo, you'll be teaching ethics and history of philosophy," another said.

"God, I hated that stuff," the first said. "Plato and Euripides. Did you notice, none of them ever shaved?"

"They say you did a great job in that wilderness parish," another priest said, a sulky blond man. It sounded like a challenge. We'll see what you're made of, he seemed to be saying. Everyone wanted to know what he was made of — these priests, Fust, Eva. And Hugo did not know himself. He was a puzzle with one piece missing. No, one piece too many.

"And that Descartes with his universal doubt," the first priest was rambling on. "What the hell can you do with a universal doubt?"

About forty students sat in the same desks that Hugo had sat in. Hugo now regretted the times when he must have appeared as bored and indifferent as these did now.

"In the eighth century a document now known as the Donation of Constantine appeared out of nowhere, it seemed, alleged to be a deed of gift from Constantine giving the pope the city of Rome and its surrounding regions. It was not until the fifteenth century that a scholar named Lorenzo Valla proved that the Donation was a fake...."

A student raised his hand, waved it impatiently.

"Yes, Bela?"

"Excuse me, Father, but it's hard to see the relevance of all this."

Several others murmured agreement. They seemed so worldly-wise compared with the students of Hugo's day, including himself.

"Forget Constantine. What about the Communists?"

"We might handle today's problems better, gentlemen, if we all knew where we came from."

"If you ask me, Father, we should suspend classes and be out there organizing and fighting for the church and the rights of the people. And when that's done we can come back and learn where we came from."

"Who gave you that idea?"

"Jeno."

The cat was out of the bag. "Jeno said." "Jeno spoke to us yesterday." "Jeno says to fight; it's the only way."

"You can't win by fighting them. They have bigger armies."

"There were ten thousand at Jeno's protest meeting on Saturday. The regime can't kill them all." Jeno was their prophet, crusading and urging revolution, a reproach to all the faint-hearted, especially the priests like Hugo.

Jeno's village was bigger than Berkos. He had a bigger church, beside apple trees, and beyond it the tombstones reflected the headlights of Hugo's car as he arrived with a warning hoot of the horn.

Inside, there was the big hug and much backslapping, like old times. Jeno threw a bottle of beer across the room, and Hugo caught it with panache. Jeno pulled out one side of his plastic collar so that it hung askew like that of Ladislaus. Then he found a pipe and held it in one hand while he came forward to shake hands with the other. They talked about the past, mostly remembering the good times. They laughed a lot. Jeno had a housekeeper, a very old woman who brought out a tray for each, and they ate heartily, the talk slowing and then falling silent until they had finished, and the mood changed imperceptibly as tension crept into the room.

"You're a hero with the students," Hugo finally said.

"Do I detect a tone of disapproval?"

"They interrupted my class yesterday. Didn't want to hear about the Donation of Constantine. They wanted to go out and fight the Communists."

"Not a bad idea, if you ask me."

"But it's not what seminaries are for."

"So what are seminaries for? To learn about the Donation of Constantine?"

"Peace and reconciliation are at the heart of our message, Jeno. Besides, the Communists are stronger."

"No, they're not stronger, Hugo. We're right, and there's nothing stronger than that."

"No one has a monopoly on right, not even the Catholic Church."

"Oh, for Christ's sake, Hugo."

"I mean it. We could learn something from them too. Look! I'm not asking you to change your ideas, just to, you know, take it easy."

"Easy be damned; we're only starting."

"I'm begging you, Jeno."

"Whose side are you on, anyway?"

"Right now, I'm on your side."

"Then do me a favor — leave me alone."

They glared at each other. It seemed a good time to stop the talk. Who knew where further words might lead? Jeno threw one more beer across to Hugo. They sat looking into the hearty fire, big logs burning through at the middle. They let their emotions sink back from the surface into their inner selves where people usually keep them hidden. They exchanged small talk about classmates and books. Jeno imitated Ladislaus one more time, scratching his head with the mouthpiece of his pipe.

"It's getting late." And indeed it was. See you soon. And take care. Yes, and you too. "You were never sensible."

"Thank God." The big rubber grin. The old bear hug. See you soon. And yes, take care.

Hugo was working on a new book. He had graduated to an old type-writer on which he plodded loudly at a table by the bed. He would show Bela — and Jeno for that matter — that the Donation of Constantine did somehow matter, that people did not arrive in a vacuum, that they were the sum of their influences, that history molded events and people into an inevitable pattern, that it was worth figuring out the pattern.

There was a slapping sound at the door, and without waiting for an invitation Ladislaus entered, animated, waving a letter.

"You did it, Hugo; by God you did it."

"Sit down, Ladislaus," Hugo said, still typing, playing it cool, "and tell me what you're talking about."

"They changed their minds — the regime. And listen to this: not only will they allow us to raise money; they are prepared to subsidize."

"That's great news, Ladislaus."

"It's better than that; it's a bloody miracle. I phoned the monsignor, but he said to turn it down."

"Why would he do that?" Hugo was now paying full attention.

"He said if we take their money we'd be in their power."

"But it's not their money. It's the people's money."

"That's what I told him."

"And he agreed?"

"Eventually. He has great confidence in you."

"I admire his judgment."

Fust had a new silver sports car, and Hugo was his passenger as they drove by a lake beside which the trees were turning gold and brown, a picture of tranquillity in the unspoiled countryside. Hugo, like Fust, was casually dressed.

"Did your friend Ladislaus get his letter?"

"Yes."

"And was he happy?"

"Yes."

"Do I detect a dark mood, Father Ovath?"

Off to the right was an elegant country club. Hugo could see that Fust savored the new car; he was but a boy in many ways. He parked under trees. They went for a walk by the lake on grounds where roses bloomed. People waved to Fust.

"Have you met my friend Ovath?"

Some of them had. Fust and Hugo had grown daring. After all, their strategy was the forging of a new spirit of cooperation between the government and the church, and Hugo was the pivot of this new relationship. Hugo was the trump card up Fust's sleeve for some future day when this whole scheme would pay off.

"You remember Ivoski?" Fust was breezy, refusing to relinquish his good mood. Hugo nodded. "Ivoski exemplifies the constant danger of corruption within the Party. But just surviving long enough one can get to be somebody, and that can be dangerous. . . ."

"There is a priest who should be removed," Hugo cut in, blurting out the words to get them said. "A very idealistic man, he could be dangerous."

"What do you mean, removed?" Fust was suddenly attentive.

"Maybe lock him up for a year."

"What's his name?"

"First, I want your word that nothing worse will happen to him."

"Who, Hugo?"

"Do I have your word?"

"Don't do this to me, Hugo." Fust's words were soft, but Hugo knew from experience this was his most deadly tone, when things were beyond words and anything could happen. "You know how things work. I don't tell you how to say Mass, all right? And the way things work, if you — if you're not cooperative, what use are you? And where does that leave me? I'd have to kill you, Hugo. God damn it, you're smart...."

"Hold it...."

"It's an amazing thing, Hugo — that our little secret isn't written down anywhere in the entire world. Think about it. The whole meaning of your life is locked up in two heads in Moscow...."

"It's not the meaning of my life."

"...And three people here at home..."

"You'll have to shoot me right now, Zoltan."

"Zoltan! You never call me Zoltan."

"I hope you don't mind." They walked by the sparkling water to their right while fat men played golf to the left, on a beautiful evening of red sunset. "Right and wrong are getting complicated, Zoltan. I am more than an experiment. And this priest's life is worth something too." Hugo gathered confidence as he spoke. "I teach ethics now, you know. And if you're going to threaten to kill me every time we disagree, you might as well do it now because, let me tell you, Zoltan, you're not God either."

"Jesus! What the fuck is happening to you, boy? You know I love you like a son...."

"Do I have your word you won't kill him?"

"My word isn't worth much, Hugo."

"It's all I have."

"You have my word. Who is it?"

"Jeno."

No sooner had Hugo spoken the word than Fust spun around in a surprisingly agile motion for a man of middle age. He pulled a gun from his pocket as he spun and fired all six rounds out over the lake. The bullets passed within inches of Hugo's head, as they were meant to do. The cracks of the gun broke the lovely stillness of the evening. Several club members, including the fat golfers, stopped in their tracks and looked in amazement.

"Jesus, Hugo, I could have killed you." Fust searched his pockets, presumably for more bullets. Finding none, he returned the gun to his pocket. "How are we ever going to fix the world, boy?"

"I'm beginning to think, Zoltan, that it's not fixable. So maybe the best we can do is not make it any worse."

"If it's any help, we knew about Jeno." They walked on, people watching them. Birds one seldom heard elsewhere were singing here; it must have become their haven since the war.

"That's the fucking rotten part. It had nothing to do with you or the Party. I thought — I, Hugo, thought Jeno needed to be put away. And now that I've told you about him, I don't think it any more."

Fust and Hugo looked intently at each other: another vague level of understanding seemed to have been reached.

"We'll treat Jeno well. You have my word."

There were threatening clouds in the sky and puddles on the road as Hugo drove back to Dunauvaros. If they harmed Jeno, Hugo would kill Fust right away without letting him grow old. He drove fiercely: he would go home and kick the world in the ass. He would be greater than Fust if he could find a scheme that would be victory for all and harm for none. He raced toward his hated little room at the seminary: if he could live with himself long enough, he would devise such a scheme and write it in a book for posterity before killing himself in remorse for being a blot on human history.

Chapter Twelve

"Look at you."

It was the first time Eva had seen him without his black clerical suit.

It was a beautiful Sunday. After Mass he had left the seminary in his usual black suit, the new sports coat and slacks hidden on the back seat of the car, blue shirt in a box. He stopped on a lonely stretch of road to make the switch. Each time a car passed he felt exposed and guilty. It was precisely the kind of dirty trick fate might play to spoil his day: sending out some innocent driver who would recognize him and have no option but to tell the world about his duplicity. He wrapped the black suit in a brown paper bag and put it in the trunk of the car. Out on the road again, he felt a different man, a new identity.

They shook hands. Eva was dressed for outdoors. As her hair cascaded when she turned, he wondered briefly why she would be interested in him.

"Come in; don't just stand there; I have everything prepared." She was excited, almost breathless. She had a basket ready — their lunch. She took a plum from a bag and held it for him. Then she kissed him on the cheek, quickly and spontaneously, standing back to observe his reaction. The touch of her lips persisted. He stood there in confusion, a welter of tumbling thoughts and possibilities. Only two hours ago he was on the altar. This was a different plane of existence. Two realities that were not meant to meet in any one person. If he stretched out his arms, she would be in them, her jutting breasts against him to squeeze and experience. Or maybe not. Maybe she would pull away, haughty and offended and disdaining him for having presumed too much. There was risk everywhere. She finished the plum herself.

"Time to go." He tried to take some initiative. He carried the basket and held the door for her. She directed him, right here, left there, country roads. She pointed to landmarks. A battle was fought there two hundred years ago. They were going to build a new factory over there, for furniture.

"Please stop," she said suddenly.

Five children were playing under a tree. She watched them for several minutes. "I just love children," she explained. "We may go on now."

But farther up the road there were more kids. She asked him to stop again, and she watched them with the same intensity. A man came to the door of a nearby house, suspicious of the car. "Drive on," she said.

She directed him into the low hills, leaving the houses behind. There were trees everywhere, overhanging the rutted road. The sun broke through the leaves in occasional bursts. She grew excited again. "Here we are."

She had a battered map of a trail that ran by a winding stream. Rocks in the water were rough stepping stones. Out-reaching branches were polished shiny from thousands of hands gripping them for support. There were dark, sinister areas and patches of lighter green where the sun stole through. He held her hand to help her over a boulder, then released it discreetly as soon as she was over. There was suspense, wondering about the eventual time when their hands would not let go. Each was leaving it to the other to be the one to hold on. There was no talk except remarks of wonder at each new revelation round a bend, at sticks carried down the stream, a gaping cave in the cliff that she would not allow him to enter because a man once went in there and never came back.

After a couple of miles they came to the waterfall, majestic, rocks hanging precariously above. One was supposed to be shaped like the face of an old man. But Hugo could not see any such face. He came down close to see where she was pointing, until their faces touched, ever so lightly, then parted. They sat on a rock. She said Paradise was like this only with more animals. He responded that there never was a Paradise; it was fabricated by dreamers.

On the way back he held her hand to help her over a fallen tree. Neither one let go afterward. The sensation carried up the arm and into the body. The imagination did the rest — never would there be again the electric sensation of that first touch. They had to let go at last because of the narrowness of the path. He guessed that perhaps the most ecstatic moment of his life had just happened. It was a cosmic joke on humankind that it should last so briefly. But humans still had a trick up their own raveled sleeves: imagination and memory could wrap the event in glory and make it last.

Now, Hugo thought, one big barrier was broken. They were not just acquaintances: they had admitted to each other that there was something more.

In a clearing there was a battered table speckled with bird droppings, which they covered with newspapers. She had sandwiches and a flask of coffee and more plums. There was a big tree with names carved and hearts pierced with primitive arrows. He waited for her to suggest that they add theirs, but she seemed not to notice it and sat there singing a soft lullaby. He was puzzled.

Another day might be a better day but that beautiful day could never be repeated — it bothered Hugo that he spoiled the best things in life by such dark thoughts. After lunch, they walked a safe distance into the forest and then stopped, thinking the same thoughts. Hugo kissed Eva. Then he thought others might be in the forest for the same reason and thus the kiss died of nervousness before it had fulfilled its promise.

Eva's house was a little bungalow. There were flowers in a tiny garden in front, monochrome in the gloom of evening. She opened the door with a big old key and let him through.

"I can't stay," he said. It was a gesture of resistance, stopping at the brink of disaster to take stock.

"Don't talk nonsense, Hugo. You're here, aren't you?" It was such a relief to him that she didn't take him seriously. "Start a fire." She went to the kitchen. Soon after, he heard her in the bathroom. Sounds of domesticity, they would grow ordinary if repeated enough. The little living room was very feminine, with cushions and soft colors and plants in glass pots and a grandfather clock ticking solemnly. One could be content or lonely here; it all depended.

He worked at building a fire of wood. Eva returned and tinkered with a record player.

"You like Beethoven?"

"I told you we don't need a fire."

"A fire is romantic. And we need romance. The whole world needs romance. And I'm warning you this minute — I'm going to sit beside you on that sofa, so brace yourself."

He lit a match and it went out. He lit several more before the balls of paper caught the pale flame, very slowly, creeping up into the wood until there was a crackle. She patted him on the back.

"I'll take your jacket." He handed it to her. He was powerless in her hands, he said to himself — it made things so much easier, he reflected wryly. He sat on the sofa and she sat beside him. She took his hand. Their heads came closer. The grandfather clock chose that moment to chime, and Hugo's head retreated, startled, causing both to laugh. They tried again, closer and closer, no hurry. They had, after all, done it already. In the woods. In a way. This was different. Safe from people, not like the woods.

"Shouldn't we talk a bit first?" he pulled away again.

"About what?"

He had no answer, so the heads approached again. Lest he escape once more she put her hands behind his head to hold him in place, and their faces came closer, lips slightly open in classic fashion, Eva was thinking, just like the movies. She couldn't imagine what Hugo was thinking. And touch. That indescribable feeling that had neither rhyme nor reason.

Everything slow and tentative and alive with wonder. The intensity growing. The bodies heaving. The breathing changing. They falling back against the soft sofa, exotic and erotic, passion growing bigger and bigger and hands now feeling here and there, more and more until they were ready to burst and had to come up for air.

"I think you're beautiful," Hugo said.

"Do you love me?"

"I think so."

"Well, Hugo Ovath, I don't think so. I'm sure." He put his arm around her shoulder, cupped her breast. They sat there absorbing the sensation.

"You know the greatest moral dilemma of all time?" he asked.

"No."

"It's how could heaven possibly be better than holding you like this for all eternity — you follow?"

"I follow."

"And the other horn of the dilemma is: Wouldn't it be worth risking hell for an opportunity like this?"

The music stopped and the magic eased up. Hugo released Eva. They took deep breaths.

"I have something to tell you," she said.

"Now?"

"When I was nineteen, I had a baby." She talked fast to get it out before he might interrupt her. "A boy. Because I wasn't married, they took him away and gave him to foster parents. You need to know — from the beginning of, you know, me-and-you, that I intend to get him back."

"Back? It's not possible. . . . "

"I'm going to the kitchen now to get supper. I hope you don't think harshly of me."

He stood and watched her go, leaving the doorway empty. Happiness here today and gone today. Many a hot night in his lonely bed, he thought, he would have crushed savagely the lips of a plain or even ugly face of imagined women animal enough to answer his immense hunger. He never dared imagine that such beautiful pouting lips would open to him, his game leg coming to mind and his rawness and lack of sophistication, he from a peasant mountainside, out of his depth.

The sound of dishes came from the kitchen. He looked to his jacket on the back of a chair; looked at the door through which Eva had left him the opportunity to make a dignified exit.

She returned with plates of food, deployed them on the coffee table, went back for the coffee. There was a mist in her blue eyes when she came back. She did not sit on the sofa but on the arm chair at the side, the tray on her knees. She asked him about love. My love, my love, he wanted to say, but did not dare to say it. He did not know what love was after so many years of philosophy and theology and stale definitions created in the head but leaving no room for the heart to speak.

"Who was the father?"

"He was killed in the war. Please don't ask too many questions."

"We have no future anyway."

"What do you mean?"

"I'm a priest. It's not allowed."

"You could leave the priesthood. You wouldn't be the first."

"It's not as simple as that."

"It can if you want it to be."

"You must take my word for now, Eva — it's not that simple."

She put down her tray, returned to the sofa, and put her hands to his face.

"Oh, Hugo, why do we make it so complicated?" She kissed him, and again they fell back on the sofa. And now Hugo wondered what she was thinking. Did she love him so totally? And how could she know?

Passion returned with minimum effort. Hugo crushed her lips, now open and going inside, wanting to love his way down into her heart. His hand back in her lap and pressed against her and she encouraging him. Hand moving out and around the curve of her thigh and caressing. Hands behind her back and the contours of her shoulder blades and holding tight never to let go this beautiful night; he could have lived five lifetimes and it might never have happened to him. Nearly everything in the world was a surprise when it happened, the good and bad; what was important was to be ready to say yes to it, the good and bad, when the surprise came.

"I love you, Eva." He would show initiative too. His hand moved back toward her breast. He could die happy; he would even risk hell if he could keep his hand there forever and the sweater removed and whatever was underneath. Little button in the middle felt through the cloth, her breath catching. Nothing could be counted the equal of this, not fame or roaring crowds or one's name in the history books — the mystery of a woman's body so long denied him. Some knew it from the time they were young. The world was unfair. All his years of wild imaginings were now real at last in his arms. It would be easier to die after that. He had some fulfillment. Someone had cared enough to offer herself, all she had, all anybody had, and to say she loved him.

"Come to bed with me, darling."

The thundering leaping crowding thoughts. Eva as his wife. Hugo putting a ring on her finger. Light kiss of joy and eyes locked in confidences. Friends and celebration. Hell, even Fust and Ladislaus offering toasts in this perfect world. Eva in white and a veil and stealing glances. Hugo later carrying her over some threshold, his limp vanished in the excitement. Husband and wife in a stone house outside some small town. Patches of flowers, him digging round them, and she telling him that he was doing it wrong. He would not care. Evenings of music such as this evening stretching ahead endlessly by endless glowing fires made with balls of paper amid banter and love, love, time for bed and ecstasy, and on an April evening two children swinging from a tree, children made by the two of them together, a fair girl with a laugh and her blue eyes.

"Come to bed," she said again.

But he hadn't time to go to bed. His hand went up under the sweater, under everything, her real body there. Fumbling fingers around the little clasp. The straps slipping away. Hands moving up and down. Difficult to breathe but he not caring. To hell with Fust, who had caught Hugo at a weak moment in his youth and idealism. This was too much to give up. Hands moved around to the front, circular motion, lightest touch, and always the catch of her breath. Something within her was stirring, he could sense it, responding to him, the outcast and vagabond and friend of no one. There must be some good in him after all, some appeal. If given a chance he could live a real life with a real identity, someone at his side each morning to call him darling. Her hands were exploring too. He was a mystery too, in his own way. This was passion that nothing in life had a right to deny.

"Please, darling — come with me."

"I can't, I can't." He leaped up as if kicked in the ass by an angel or a devil. It was not the thought of Fust that rushed in to strangle his wild wish. It was the thought of the seminary. His mind raced, harking back to Ladislaus and talk of sacrifice and the barrier he and others built around the grail of celibacy, the great glory of the church through thick and thin, no concession or reprieve. No ledger recorded the days and nights of struggle, proof every time he won a victory that there was a God. The arguments in the books could not compare with that. It was not so easy to shed the heroic image that had appealed to his youth and dedication and been placed on a pedestal. Not to mention Fust reminding him over his shoulder: we want our priest to be the best priest in the country. "Sorry, I just can't do it," he sounded so sad.

"What?"

"It's a commitment I made long ago...."

"It's a stupid commitment." Eva was standing too, adjusting her bra and fastening it. "What right have they to deny you?" She had stumbled on the ironic heart of the problem. Hugo was not Gyula; he was not Ladislaus or old Bishop Illyes. He should not be bound by their rules. "The priests who give up love are not men; they're only half-men. I have seen them. You're not like that. I could feel that you were a man."

"You know nothing about them, Eva." He felt obliged to say the simple truth. Were he to go into the bedroom with her, it would not be because he was more a man than Gyula or Jeno.

"The church is finished, darling. Get out before something happens to you." There was a great wistfulness about her, hands touching Hugo's face, drawing him to her again; she would not give up easily, her lips hot and hard to let go. It was impossible to sort out the confusion of thoughts just when he was on the threshold of all his dreams — all that remained was to open the door. "We could go away and be married," she said. "We could live in the south, far from here; no one would know or ever find us."

"In a small house outside some town," he was wilting again, feeding the dream. "Preferably beside a little babbling river. You're not the only one has been thinking about it."

"And I would search for my boy and get him back."

This caused him to break loose from her again, turning to the window and looking out on the quiet street. He wondered briefly whether the boy was the result of one thoughtless frenzied night or a love that had absorbed the years of her freshness.

"But he's not mine."

"Do you not love me, Hugo?"

"If I were free, my love, I'd marry you with a song in my heart." Of course it was a dream, and even dreams were flawed on closer examination. The boy would be the flaw in Hugo's dream, and he could live with it. "Yes, and I'd help you search for him. The boy. I'd teach him to play soccer — with my lame leg and all. And we'd go hiking by the waterfall and watch him throwing stones in the river. And in a short time, Eva, in that perfect world, we'd give him a brother and a sister, whatever he wanted." He paused, looking down on her. "If only we were free."

She picked up the dishes, took them to the kitchen, all business as she herself would say, and returned with a scowl.

"You're a coward; that's what you are."

"Maybe." Hugo picked up his jacket, backed toward the door. He could still turn it around, he thought one more time. He could take her in his arms and say he had changed his mind. Except that he had no mind to change. Only the mind of Fust and Ladislaus and the doddering monsignor. He was programmed by others since he was twenty; his youth was passing without ever a chance to do one spontaneous thing. There was no room for anger or mistakes or passion of any kind, just day after endless day of beware, beware. "I had a wonderful day," he managed to say.

"I had a wonderful day too." She was fighting against being angry with him, and this drew him to her even more. It might have been easier if she were angry. The fire had died to embers. Cheap symbolism, he thought. Devoid of substance, his mind readily straddled every passing symbol, or so he saw himself at that low moment. At the door he leaned to kiss her on the cheek, ever so lightly, while she held her face sideways, saying nothing.

It was after midnight when Hugo drove up the crunchy gravel driveway to the seminary. As the car swung round it illuminated the entire building. His guilty imagination working feverishly; he envisaged the light entering every darkened window, and the men inside, restless on their hard beds, no doubt knowing it was he and that only lust would keep a healthy young priest out so late.

As he padded stealthily down the dimly lit corridor it was a shock to see a sliver of light coming from his own room. Ladislaus was sitting in the spare chair. The pipe was dead — more symbolism, Hugo thought. He remained seated. There was a touch of reproach in his voice.

"You're out very late, Hugo."

"Is something wrong?"

"It's Jeno."

"Damn, what did he do now?" Hugo's first reaction was relief: his own skin was still safe. Then came the sinking feeling, the well-cultivated guilt.

As the days passed he had begun to hope the regime would give Jeno some miraculous reprieve. Hell, let him go out and cause trouble; stupid old innocent Jeno could never make a dent in the mighty Communist machine. Giving Jeno freedom to be a nuisance would prove how magnanimous the Party was. Fust would arrange something clever for Hugo's sake — he and Fust went back a long way, and a quaint affection had grown over the years, though on bad days Hugo thought it had grown more like a tumor than a grace. Jeno, meanwhile, had not helped: raging against the regime and drawing ever bigger crowds.

"They've taken him."

"He was so damn imprudent. I tried to talk to him."

"I know."

Hugo took two beers from a bottom drawer. He put one in front of Ladislaus on the desk. Ladislaus shook his head with a hint of disapproval. Hugo drank, straining to be normal.

"You'll have to do something."

"This is different, Ladislaus. Dealing with money is one thing. . . ."

"What's the name of that man in town?"

"Madach."

"That's it — Madach. You'll have to talk to him." He got up to go. He picked up the bottle of beer, giving Hugo a bleary eye and a curt nod. Hugo wanted Ladislaus to stay and talk about Jeno. He wanted to say how much he loved Jeno. But it was already the early hours of morning. Lust slinked out through the open window as Hugo cried inwardly, having long since smothered the capacity for tears, but never loving Jeno more than on that night when his betrayal had come home to roost.

Jeno was in some stinking cell, waiting for the cold verdict of prison or death. The thrust forward thighs of his long-ago girl were now of little account. Or perhaps they were a solace. A cherished hour out of a lifetime that carried a balm, an invisible treasure to wrap in memory and take to the grave. Or was Jeno sustained by some greater vision that made it all easy and glowing? Or was it a bleak God keeping his distance and taunting with doubts and regrets as Job and some of the saints allegedly suffered? If so, Hugo wondered what kind of iron man Jeno was. Iron of the will holding him unbending before anything except the one God far out there and seemingly paying no notice — that strength was greater than that of Fust.

And a greater dream than Fust's if one could believe in it. Hugo still envied Jeno: envied something in him that helped him carry the heavier case without even noticing, way back then. If he were ever to get acquainted with that big God, it would be from men like Jeno, giving up the beckoning girls and their pouting mouths, then making some absurd leap of self-denial when all the common sense in the world said grab what you can before it's too late.

Chapter Thirteen

They sat in the same dining room in the old monastery where they had asked Hugo to become a priest.

"It's a sort of symbolic thing," Fust said. "What is it — ten, fifteen years? We've come a long way, my boy. And now, out of the blue..." Even the table was the same. And on the other side of the table was the man from Moscow, and down at the end Ivoski was still eating like a horse. They had all grown older. They were a special little club with special knowledge. Hugo wondered briefly what compelled Fust to let the uncouth Ivoski in on such a spectacular secret.

"Not out of the blue, Zoltan."

"This letter about Eva. Eva is a lovely girl. I admire your taste, Hugo. But in a world of constant upheaval like ours you will quickly forget her."

"Women, Hugo," Ivoski stopped chomping to make his contribution. "Listen to me now. That first — you know — sure it's great, but after you get tired of humping one...What I'm saying is..." Hugo waited for Fust to pull out a gun and shoot Ivoski, but nothing happened. They had indeed grown older.

"We admire what you've done, my boy." Fust was conciliatory.

"It's a failure, Zoltan." Hugo, for his part, felt melancholy, as if mourning the death of a favorite dream.

"No, it's not. We have plans. You won't always be in that seminary. They'll make you a bishop...."

"You have forbidden them to appoint bishops — remember?" The man from Moscow sat taciturn as he did years before. When future historians wrote his biography the most they would be able to say was that he, too, was a symbol of something, though no one could figure out what.

"Don't worry, we'll make an exception for you."

"Sorry, Zoltan, the answer is no."

"What do you propose to do?"

"I told you in the letter: I propose to marry Eva."

"There's just one thing wrong with that. Eva doesn't want to marry you."

"God damn you, Zoltan," Hugo jumped up, "what have you done to her." Ivoski jumped up too. Though he must now be sixty, Ivoski still saw himself as the enforcer.

"Easy, boy, easy," Fust was saying. "You can't imagine what a blow your letter was. So unexpected. Just when success was within reach. Even Moscow has been showing unaccustomed interest. And now, all you want to do is run away from your commitment and get married."

"I want to talk to Eva." Hugo had agreed to help her get her son back. And they had planned a son and daughter of their own who would play in a garden of sunshine and flowers under a perfect sky on a day that would have no evening.

"I had come to regard you as a brother, Hugo."

"I want to see Eva."

"Of course."

Eventually they filed out of the monastery into the same courtyard where Bishop Illyes was executed. It was a picture of peace on a beautiful day. Ivy had grown back on the wall — they must have found a more suitable place for their executions, Hugo thought.

"Where's Jeno?" Hugo asked.

Fust, instead of answering, performed a grotesque charade. He marched to where the firing squad stood to shoot the bishop. He raised an imaginary gun, shouting "Fire!" and then "Bang!" He grabbed his chest as if he had been shot. For a moment he stood looking up at the sky. Ivoski laughed loudly while the man from Moscow looked morosely at Fust as if he were a fool. Then just as suddenly Fust returned soberly to Hugo.

"That's what I wanted to tell you, Hugo. About Father Jeno. We are taking him out of circulation for a while."

"I want to know where."

"I can't tell you."

"I insist on knowing."

"Cut it out — or I'll lock you up along with him." Fust was angry now, walked away again across the courtyard, back and forth, crazy or merely volatile or merely an actor. After so many years Hugo could not be sure. Then back he came, full of intensity, layered with goodwill, speaking quietly.

"You make me say things, Hugo. Listen — we'll get it all fixed eventually. We'll clean up all the crap and the sin; we'll redeem the whole fucking thing and make the world perfect as the day it was new."

"No, you won't. You'll make it worse."

Fust now allowed himself to be amused by Hugo's depression. "Yes, we will."

Even when he hated Fust most, Hugo envied him his energy and resilience; he wanted to be strong and convinced like Fust.

In full daylight the flowers in front of Eva's house were more or-dinary and less mysterious than in the magic gloom of twilight — another symbol of something so obvious it doesn't need symbolism, Hugo thought grimly as he knocked on her door. She opened imme-diately as if she had been waiting inside for his knock. She looked tired, wan. There was no smile or gladness. She looked at him with an appeal that said, Don't be hard on me; don't expect answers. She stood aside for him to enter, and he did. She led him back to the little living room, scene of such brief but magnificent happiness.

"Coffee?"

"If you have some made."

She went and got it. Two mugs on a tray. She had that ready too; she had been warned he was coming. He sat on the sofa, and she sat on the chair.

"Is it true, Eva?"

"What?"

"You know well."

"Yes, it's true."

"Did they threaten you?"

"No."

"The truth, Eva?"

"It was a mistake, Hugo. You're a priest."

"That didn't bother you before." It was possible Fust told her about Hugo's real significance to the Party. She was smart enough to know that his was not a personal friendship with Fust. And she knew the Communists would be delighted to see a priest defecting, especially a big-shot, high-visibility priest like Hugo. She had never questioned him, and he would not have told her. Unless, of course, they were married.

"I wasn't thinking before."

"So what started you thinking?"

"Please, Hugo. What does it matter what they told me?" There was only one plausible explanation: they'd told her he was a Judas who'd betrayed his people.

"It would matter if you loved me."

"Not even then." She sat demurely with her knees sideways, a little handkerchief in her hand in case she might need it.

"Oh, my God — they told you a big one, whatever it was." Some day he would kill Fust. He would lure him to some lonely forest where he would torture him until he spilled the beans about Eva. Then he would kill him. Or maybe not: there was, quite likely, a peace in death to which Fust was not entitled.

"Please, Hugo."

"Remember the plans we made? A little house and you getting to know your son again and I teaching him soccer."

He put out a hand to touch her arm, but she pulled back. She stood, took his cup, and put it on the tray with her own.

"Please go now."

"And I teaching him soccer." Hugo backed away toward the door. "With my lame leg. But I could have done it, you know, by God I could. Love can do anything. A little house with flowers growing wild down to the river. Well, at least a stream, I'd settle for a stream...."

She didn't stand at the door to watch him go but closed it behind him.

Chapter Fourteen

The discontent and anger and betrayal and fear had been simmering for years, then for months became a fierce rumbling ferment, and turned to open revolt on an October day in 1957.

At lunchtime, about thirty priests and seminarians listened to the radio in the big bare seminary recreation room. They understood well enough the frosty, distant British accent on the BBC Foreign Service — more trustworthy than local stations.

"For years the cauldron has been simmering, non-Communists against Communists; then new Communists against old Communists. Today it became, by all accounts, an open revolution. . . ."

Ladislaus sat amid the students, intense and worried. It was a popular uprising, the announcer was saying, unplanned and uncoordinated. It was triggered by the intelligentsia, authors, artists, and university students. They had, more or less peacefully, rid the country, some months ago, of the disreputable Rakos, Party hack until he became prime minister, the man most responsible for the forced work camps, collectivization, repression of free speech. But when Rakos was replaced by Paul Gerton, another Moscow puppet, everyone marched, which was nothing new.

What was new was the general agreement that there would be fighting. An unspoken assumption, but because everyone agreed there was no alternative, it was bound to happen. It was, Hugo thought, the way most wars started, when people resigned themselves to them.

Every group had points and programs, the radio man was saying. But when the metaphorical man in the street was asked, he seemed to have little positive plan, except that he would like a freer and better life, and he made it sound like a reasonable request.

"In the corridors of power, sources say, heads are rolling," the radio man said.

Hugo quietly left the recreation room. When he reached his own room, he locked the door behind him. Only he and Ladislaus had private phones. Hugo needed one because he was growing prominent, dealing with the regime on behalf of the leaderless diocese, able to cajole money and other favors for people. He was, after all, the priest who had stopped the Party in its tracks in Berkos even before there was widespread revolt.

"May I speak to Mr. Fust?"

"Who is this?"

"Please, it's urgent — when do you expect him?"

"If you give me your name, perhaps someone else can help you." Whether the heads were rolling literally or figuratively, Hugo had the strong impression that radical change was in progress. He said he would call later. He slipped back quietly to the recreation room.

The young and old were marching, the foreign voice said. They were good-natured and triumphant. They had gathered at the Writers' Union and were now marching in the direction of Union Square. There were tens of thousands. There were no police in sight, the radio man kept saying. More sensational still, groups of young soldiers in uniform could be seen marching with the crowds. The people had signs and slogans and shouted out their excitement, at times drowning out the radio man.

Deep in the big seminary the bell rang for class. The students groaned and protested. Ladislaus turned off the radio. "It's nothing. They will get nowhere." He dismissed the marchers with a wave of his pipe.

In the classroom the students were in no mood for Hugo's brand of ethics.

"This is what we've been waiting for," Bela said. "Drive out the Communists."

"You're forgetting, Bela; you're forgetting that those are Communists out there." Hugo had trouble liking Bela, perhaps because he was too much like Jeno, and one Jeno was enough in any world. "Communists against Communists. All they are asking for is a new brand."

"It's a first step," another student said. They were elated so long as the status quo was toppled and trampled on.

"If the Russians were gone, there wouldn't be many Communists."

"If only Jeno were here." They mentioned Jeno constantly, their

hero and inspiration. In the end they argued among themselves, ig-
noring Hugo, whom they regarded as at best above it all if not a total
political fuddy-duddy and ethical fiasco. What they wanted was revolt
and blood. They were young men from stubborn countrysides where
everything had to be won by physical conquest far from the smart talk
and political connections that got things done in cities.

After class, they raced back to the recreation room, Hugo limping
behind them. Ladislaus and the other priests were already there. The
entire country was at a standstill awaiting the outcome.

There were fifty thousand people in the square now. The peasant
poet Peter Hages stood on the pedestal of a statue and read a ten-
point resolution from the students. The people listened at first, but in
their exhilaration it was not talk they wanted but action.

They turned their attention to a statue of Stalin, twenty-four feet
high. The inscription said, "To the Great Stalin, from the Grateful
People." Workers from a nearby factory brought acetylene torches to
cut through the bronze. There was growing amusement and finally
pandemonium as the statue came tumbling down. The excitement
in the square was reflected in the seminary recreation room. And in
homes around the country, Hugo was sure, that same hysteria was
being fueled.

Stalin's two giant feet were all that was left on the pedestal, the
announcer was saying, while the students in their elation climbed all
over the fallen idol.

Hugo returned to his room and made another fruitless phone call.
The trouble with Fust's seat-of-the-pants style was that it left everyone else in a quandary when a crisis arose, and in Fust's world crises
arose with numbing regularity. Fust might be dead now — it was no
secret how quickly people disappeared — and Fust had never said what
to do in the case of his untimely death. Or timely death for that matter. His death is long past timely, Hugo thought, allowing himself a
little macabre humor, all the more macabre because he could never
share the joke with anyone. He would write it in his diary, he decided, eventually in his memoirs. If he could stay alive long enough,
he would tell it all.

The simplest way would be to make no decisions. Let them revolt.
Let whoever was strongest or smartest win. Let the future go to hell.
Hugo felt tired.

At dinner, Ladislaus rang the little hand bell. "Let us praise

God and celebrate this historic moment," he intoned. "Benedicamus Domino."

"Deo gratias," they responded with satisfaction.

Ladislaus passed the big platter of roast beef to the priest beside him. "I'm too excited. We'll have plenty of time for eating later," Ladislaus commented.

"I think you're overestimating what's going on out there," Hugo suggested.

"Could be," Ladislaus said. "But it could also be a chance to drive them out. To break the whole darned Communist stranglehold."

"There would be a lot of bloodshed."

"There are times when bloodshed is inevitable, Hugo. Just as it was on the cross. On second thought, would you pass me that platter? God forgive me but I'm starving."

The radio in the recreation room kept drawing them all back, the magic link with momentous reality outside. But, according to the radio man, the carnival was becoming ugly. The hated secret police had arrived in force in front of the Radio Building. The jovial crowd had turned angry and thrown stones. The military police retaliated with tear gas. Shots were fired. A worker was killed. The rest was rumor, the commentator said, about how many were killed, and on which side. One thing was certain: the turmoil was growing. Flags were waved defiantly. Someone was waving a flag of the regime but with the Russian emblem cut out, leaving a hole in the middle. A flag with a hole in it might be appropriate for many countries, Hugo said to Bela, who was not amused.

"You said it would come to nothing," Bela taunted. "What do you say now?"

"The revolution has come to Dunauvaros," two students rushed in. They had heard shots and shouting and saw trucks passing with soldiers.

The students rushed out to see. Hugo too went out. Night had fallen on the town. There was a silver brightness where the moon was hidden behind ruptured clouds. The cathedral's tall spires were floodlit as usual down by the railway station. Lights shone lazily in windows. It looked like a sleeping town until the night was broken by the shouts. They could be shouts of anger or merely elation, people celebrating or being killed.

Then there were shots, quick after each other. Sometimes shots were fired in the air. Hugo hoped that was all.

In the middle of the night there was a loud knocking on Hugo's door. He opened one eye. It was dark as pitch. "Who's there?"

Light from the corridor showed Ladislaus coming in. He was wearing a red shirt.

"You'd better get up, Hugo."

"What time is it?"

"There are men downstairs who want to see you."

Ladislaus went off flopping in his slippers. Hugo, in his pajamas, got out of bed, scratched his head, and looked out the window as if measuring chances of escape. He sat on the bed; it was easier to do nothing. But Ladislaus returned, wearing his rumpled soutane.

"What do they want, Ladislaus?"

"They wouldn't say." Ladislaus led the way into a dim room in the basement. Six rebels were standing by the wall, in their working clothes but carrying guns. Hugo guessed the guns were not even loaded. The leader stepped forward, a wide man about forty.

"We're sorry to disturb you," he said.

"What is it you want?" Hugo asked.

"The people are in revolt, as you must know. Most of them are not Communists, Father. They will all be killed unless, well, unless there is someone to organize them. We hoped you would lead us."

Ladislaus pulled out his pipe and lit it, looking excited, almost happy. Four rebels took this as permission to light cigarettes. When Ladislaus sat at a long table, two of the rebels sat facing him. They believed that in the seminary they were dealing with friends, because the priests always belonged to the people.

"Lead you?" Hugo was surprised. "I'm a priest, not a revolutionary."

"You did it at Berkos."

"This is different. As you said, they are all going to get killed."

"We have no one else, Father," he said. "We need the church to unite us. That's how it has always been."

"I'm from Berkos," a peasant said. "I told them about what you did there." Hugo did not recognize him. Yet he had lived on in this young man's memory and was talked about at meetings, at work, and in houses. It was something short of immortality, but it was a way of living on as long as memory lasted.

"What time?"

They shook his hand and were excited. They outlined their plans. At the door they put their caps on their heads and quickly became dark shadows among the trees.

"I'm proud of you," Ladislaus said.

"You're as bloodthirsty as the rest of them, Ladislaus." He patted the older man on the back. They drank tea in the kitchen because sleep had disappeared. Hugo meanwhile fumbled for a way to keep faith with the vanished Fust.

On a gloomy, cloudy morning Hugo was among the leaders of a rambling march down the main street of Dunauvaros to the cathedral of the tall spires. The people brought to the occasion more enthusiasm and bravado than order. Many carried flags and posters. There was a brass band, but the shouting and cheering of the people were louder.

Behind the leaders, the body of the man killed the previous day was carried aloft on a big wooden door. His wife walked beside the door wailing and holding the man's dead hand.

The march had been banned. In Cathedral Square the special forces and army and secret police were arrayed in daunting numbers behind an iron wall of tanks.

The demonstrators placed the corpse on a platform. Women put flowers around it, red roses. Several people made speeches. They said the Russians must go home and the secret police must be disbanded. It was hard to say who was allied with whom. Everyone had a cause, but the overarching, unifying cause was to get Russia off everybody's back.

"...Father Hugo Ovath, who defied the old regime in Berkos at a time when no one else dared to speak up, and won a sensational victory for the people..."

The crowd applauded, and Hugo limped forward in his long black soutane — that day at least he was a priest. He started slowly. The crowd was restless. They had heard enough speeches and wanted action. Hugo had a mind to give them not action but hope. Hope had been a substitute for action throughout history and throughout the world, and sometimes when hope grew wings and took flight people saw that action was not always necessary, especially the kind of action that led to killing.

He drew them in as he said things that touched their lives. His confidence grew, and he assured them they were a chosen people, and this was their chosen time. The church would be with them, as it always had been in times of trouble. And he, Hugo, would be with them too.

Grand old classical buildings rose in russet brick around the square, shops and offices, but that day Hugo could see soldiers at every window and their guns pointing in his direction. But, caught up in this historic moment, he knew he was safe. He could not die until something more happened, some culmination. He did not know when that destiny would fall on him, but he knew it was not today. He found it a strange intoxication to realize that every single person in the square was deceived about him. No actor had ever given such a performance. Fust would be proud: picking Hugo was one of Fust's finest achievements, or so Hugo thought, lifted up. And over there in the crowd he saw Ladislaus, a black hat on his head like a Hollywood priest, hand shading his eyes because he was looking into the sun.

"Only a beginning has been made. There will be many a broken heart, many a stab of pain, before people realize that the old ways are gone and that they are flame of the new fire, and the future will be cities of gold and countryside of green and laughing people waving. . . ."

When he finished speaking, they cheered and waved their flags with holes in the middle. He raised his hands for silence. The day's work is not yet finished, he told them. "We will now present our demands to City Hall."

The tanks and soldiers stood between the platform and City Hall. The people in a great surging mass closed in around Hugo and the other leaders. But after only a few steps they were confronted by the soldiers, and their commander shouted through a bullhorn: "Stop where you are!"

The crowd roared its defiance and pressed forward. The commander realized he was about to be overrun. He called on the tanks to move forward. "Fire!" he shouted through his bullhorn. For long seconds then the tumult stood still as everyone waited for whatever would happen next. But nothing did. The tanks did not move. The soldiers at the tall windows held their fire despite frantic orders from the commander.

The turret of a tank opened slowly and a soldier's head emerged. The people realized they would not be massacred. A great shout of triumph went up, people surging forward and pushing the commander aside. Some climbed on the tanks and consorted with the soldiers.

A little man came forward with a camera, taking Hugo's picture again and again until Hugo lurched after him: "Get out of here or I'll break your neck."

Then Ladislaus emerged from the crowd and grabbed Hugo by the arm.

"You all right, Hugo?"

"Go home, Ladislaus, for God's sake. They need you back at the seminary."

They were interrupted by the siren of an ambulance entering the square, lights flashing. It moved so recklessly fast, some protesters grew suspicious and tried to block it. When it struck a protester, the crowd dragged the driver out and beat him mercilessly.

The ambulance, they quickly saw, was full of guns, which were quickly grabbed by men in the crowd. This in turn caused the men at the upper windows to open fire. Several people fell dead or injured. The men in the square shot back at the high windows. Soon it was a pitched battle. The crowd set the ambulance on fire. There was chaos everywhere, people crying out in pain and fear. The majestic cathedral looked moodily down. Only the tanks remained unaccountably silent.

Hugo came from the direction of the cathedral carrying a wounded youth in his arms. He searched until he found the photographer, held up the boy for the camera. "You wanted a picture. Here's a picture." The little photographer, scared of Hugo's anger, took the picture, again and again.

Hugo saw Ladislaus standing nearby and looking lost. He handed Ladislaus the boy.

"Here, take him somewhere."

Hugo tried again to reach Fust. Now no one was answering the phone. The fear that grabbed him was fear of the unknown. He was on a strange, stormy sea without a compass.

As he returned to the square he walked smack into a man who had been lynched in front of a butcher shop. The man's hands were tied behind his back. One shoe was missing. He was young, with a simple face hanging expressionless. He was wearing the jacket of a once-blue uniform. He seemed dead. A crowd of people had gathered, standing back and observing, most in ill-concealed horror.

"Good God, what are you doing?"

"He's a member of the secret police," someone said. "Aren't you Father Ovath?" a woman said with admiration. The dead man was momentarily forgotten. "It's Father Ovath; it's Father Ovath," she said triumphantly to the crowd.

"He was coming over to our side, but they wouldn't listen to him," another woman was sobbing. "I told them, but they wouldn't listen."

"Whoever did it, cut him down," Hugo said. No one moved. "Cut him down, I say." They stood like statues. It wasn't defiance. They were too afraid or too horrified. Hugo had little doubt that whoever did it had safely escaped.

Hugo entered the butcher's shop. He returned with a chair and a long butcher's knife. A woman held the chair while Hugo grimly cut down the dead man. The photographer took more pictures, the flash popping, as Hugo held the dead man in his arms, offered him around to anyone who might take him. But no one moved. Hugo then took the body into the shop and placed it on the butcher's block.

He left them standing there stricken dumb and headed for the seminary, walking wearily up the steep hill past the statue where he and Jeno had stopped to rest as they took each other's measure on the day they first met.

Ladislaus was alone drinking tea at the head table of the refectory. Hugo joined him.

"Bela is gone."

"Gone?"

"With the insurgents. He won't be coming back." Ladislaus sounded defeated.

"It's not your fault. He wants to die for the people. It's an old Christian tradition." A student came running.

"They want Father Ovath. The soldiers do." The soldiers had not waited for an invitation. They filled the hall, guns in their hands.

"I'm Ovath," Hugo said to the officer, a veteran with a loose, lined face.

"A member of the secret police was hanged by the mob tonight. We have information that you were present."

"I arrived afterward. The man was already dead." The seminarians were standing at a distance. This too was part of their education — the real world.

"Have you any witnesses?" the officer asked.

"What are you insinuating, Jack?" Ladislaus stepped in front of the officer. "Why would he need witnesses?"

"Who are you?"

"I'm in charge here, and you're on consecrated ground. I think you should be more circumspect with your language."

"There were many witnesses." Hugo was eager to keep Ladislaus out of trouble. "Naturally I didn't know them."

"Then you have no witnesses."

"This is an outrage," Ladislaus blustered.

"Look," Hugo said. "Whoever gave you your information can tell you I'm the one who cut down the body."

"One thing is sure: someone did it. Am I right?" The officer's kind face belied his abrasive manner. He would not go on until Hugo nodded. "And someone will have to pay, isn't that fair?" Again he waited, playing his cat-and-mouse game.

"If that somebody was guilty, yes," Hugo qualified.

"Everyone out on the streets was guilty."

"I disagree entirely."

"I didn't ask your opinion." He took Hugo by the shoulders and turned him around, then pushed him roughly down the corridor as if trying to provoke a reaction. It was dark outside. Another soldier helped Hugo into the back of a truck. This soldier gave Hugo what he interpreted as a look of compassion. In a quick spiritual somersault Hugo resolved again to be the best priest on earth, at least until he got out of jail, or wherever he was being taken — if, that is, he ever got out. He noted the irony that it was easier to be the best priest on earth when things were going badly than when they were going well. It was something he would put in his diary. It was easier to be a good Communist, however, when things were going well.

Dungeons, Hugo concluded, were the same the world over. The same dark and damp and smell of urine and the same clang of lock on heavy door. He stood motionless until his eyes grew accustomed to the darkness. Then he saw a figure, an older man in the corner, sitting on the floor and propped against the wall. He moved closer and peered.

"So they caught you," the older man said.

"Don't worry; we'll soon be out of here." It was bravado speaking — this time Fust might have gone down, and Hugo would sink with him.

"We'll never get out." There was no panic in the old man's voice. He was a man of few words, but when the night got cold he suggested they sit side by side for heat. And indeed Hugo felt surprising heat coming from the old body and hoped the old man was getting something in return.

The loud unlocking of the door jarred them awake. Two soldiers shone lights in their faces and then handcuffed Hugo without a word.

"Don't show fear," the old man said, still hunched in the corner. "Don't give them that satisfaction."

"You'll be out soon," Hugo said, and the old man snorted.

They emerged into the sunlight of the courtyard of the former monastery. It was winter and there was no sunshine, and no flowers. For a brief moment Hugo was convinced they were going to kill him, and this was Fust's sick sense of humor closing the circle where it began. Instead, he was led to the dining room.

The wrinkled officer was sitting at the wooden table. Without a word he signaled to the soldiers to remove the handcuffs. Puzzled, he searched Hugo's face for a clue. He dialed a number and handed the phone to Hugo.

"Ovath here."

Hugo was not surprised to hear Fust at the other end. "Where are you?" Hugo asked angrily. "Why the fuck are you never there when I need you?" When Hugo made his deal of a lifetime he had not bargained for all this abuse, guns and arrests and cold dungeons, and least of all the chirpy bonhomie of Fust on the line. All the better that these soldiers were listening: it was time to spread the humiliation around. Let the soldiers figure out who was who and who was king in this little jungle — Hugo called Fust a few more names while Fust tried to soften him.

"If your thugs let me go," Hugo was saying. "Maybe this afternoon? ... No, listen! What you suggest is not consistent with being the best priest on earth.... Yes.... And one more thing. There's a man — he was with me in your dungeon last night. I want him released within the hour. . . . No, now — I want you to say it to the thug who seems to be in charge here. Come here, you," he said to the officer. The officer took the phone. He mumbled in response to Fust's instructions. By the time he hung up he was a thoroughly obsequious public servant.

"I didn't know," he began.

"You didn't know what?"

"Whatever it is you want, sir, just let me know."

Hugo opted to walk back to the seminary, striding as grandly as his limp would allow, attracting attention. Before he reached home he sensed something wrong. Not such a great feat, he told himself, when all around so much was wrong. Still, he realized he could smell trouble better than average citizens. Trouble and he were cousins and knew each other well.

On a refectory table lay the dead body of Bela. There was blood on his chest in dark blotches. The soldiers had opened fire and killed a dozen people, a student explained.

"He can thank Jeno for this," Hugo said quietly so the students would not hear.

"I don't want you saying anything bad about Jeno." Ladislaus was vehement.

He often ate at this table, Hugo recalled, and so did I. Now there was blood on it. Students came by and touched Bela, held a hand to his face, cold already. Many of the students cried. Bela was already a success: he had turned the students against the regime for the rest of all their lifetimes. He had always been so impatient in class. Perhaps he felt deep within that he had limited time. Anyone who is going to die at twenty has no time for the Donation of Constantine. You need a whole lifetime. But that begged the question of what exactly was a whole lifetime.

"I will visit Madach this afternoon."

"God bless you, Hugo," Ladislaus said.

Chapter Fifteen

The streets of the city were full of confusion, just like Dunauvaros. He parked his car when he could drive no farther. Trams and trucks were overturned nearby, burnt-out shells. He left his black breviary conspicuous on the front seat: it might at least make the marauders feel guilty.

Around the corner there was a roadblock: barrels and planks and armed men crouching. He worried about the slip of paper in his pocket.

"Where are you going?" a young man asked.

"To visit a family. The mother is ill." He had become an accomplished liar, though that was not how he saw it.

The way one fashioned the truth determined the success or failure of one's mission. Guns were blunt instruments and could not accomplish everything. Thoughts ruled the world, and every thought could be squeezed and flattened and thrown in the air and caught coming down, shaped in short to suit the occasion, a prism for the truth.

"We'll have to search you," the young man was saying.

"Why?"

"You might not be what you appear to be."

If they searched they would find the list. He had started with forty-five names, leaders and others dangerous to the regime. He cut the list to thirty and finally to nineteen. Doubts kept rising. It was not just their names on paper — it was their lives. Not that they would be killed. The Sandor episode was a sad mistake. They would be more like Jeno, taken for safekeeping. Jeno was probably having a grand old time in some country-club camp. Hugo hoped that instead of sowing subversion Jeno was passing the time with toy mice and rubber turds to keep the other inmates content.

"Let him through," an older man came forward. "We heard the

secret police were going around dressed as priests," he explained to Hugo. "But you don't look like one." He was looking intently at Hugo. "Be careful," he advised the priest.

When Hugo looked back, several men were standing observing him. They wore civilian clothes so it would be impossible to know if someone were following him. He twice circled Party headquarters, zigging and zagging up and down side streets, before he was reassured. Two tanks squatted ominously in a courtyard. Soldiers loitered on the steps. Violence had subsided for the moment, but hostility was in the air.

Inside, the old desk was gone. Where Eva used to sit. Where they first talked. There was no song that was their song. No favorite restaurant. There were few traces. They did not even engrave their names on that tree by the river. And here, where she made her first impression, her desk was gone and everything changed. Her name was never mentioned — Fust refused to answer any questions about her, but Hugo had a dream that before he killed Fust some future sunny day he would extract from him by torture the reason behind Eva's change of attitude toward him.

An old man in uniform referred Hugo to a young woman, and she referred him to a handsome bureaucrat of sixty who said his name was Salus. He was impeccably groomed, with silver hair and smart suit. He sat with his elbows on an empty desk, his fingertips touching, restrained but friendly. Hugo said he had business with Mr. Fust.

"There are terrible things happening, Mr. Ovath," Salus said. There was no chair to sit on, so Hugo stood in front of Salus's desk.

"That is what I wanted to talk to Mr. Fust about."

"What exactly?"

"Some ringleaders in my town that I think the Party should know about."

"You want to turn them in?"

"If I could see Zoltan Fust..."

"They could be executed."

"As you say, there are terrible things happening."

"How many?"

"Nineteen."

"Not counting their wives and kids?"

"Are you mocking me, sir?"

"A fine priest you are. A traitor to your own people."

"They are leading the people to bloodshed."

"A Judas." Salus had never raised his voice or separated his poised fingertips. "When you should be ready to die for them — even if they are stupid; even, God help us, if they are on the wrong side. Are you really a priest?"

"I really am," Hugo was surprised at his own humility. For what it was worth it was true. But it was a damaged truth that he now realized he couldn't fix. He could not be transformed into a good and believing priest just by willing it, just because Fust was gone. There were no longer any dramatic conversions like Paul the Jew on the road to Emmaus. He was destined to play this sordid part. Out of this pit he could eventually climb to some eminence; he had the stuff in him to do that. But meanwhile, crippled though his soul might be, he truly was a priest.

"I expect you have a list in your pocket?" When Hugo did not answer, Salus pressed on, "Take it out." Hugo took the folded yellow page from his pocket. Salus made room on his desk. "Now tear it into small pieces."

"You'll answer for this," Hugo tried for a comeback. "You're interfering in affairs you know nothing about." But after several seconds of matching wills with Salus he tore the paper into small pieces. He then collected them and put them in his pocket. It was the abyss of humiliation. He could not explain, to Salus or Fust or even himself, why he had allowed this trickster to trap him into such a pit.

"I won't ask your name. I'd rather not know." It wasn't kindness; it was meant to be cruelty.

"Ovath, sir," Hugo said, gathering up his fallen dignity. "Hugo Ovath. Remember it, because some day you'll read about it in the history books — providing we all live long enough — and then you'll be able to understand."

The man solemnly observed Hugo crossing the vestibule.

As he limped along the crowded street, the young man who had previously stopped him did it again. A ubiquitous young man, Hugo reflected from the depths of his misery — the rebels had moved their roadblock.

"What is it now?"

"You are to wait here," the young man said. "Would you do that? Promise you won't go running off?" Without waiting for an answer he went running down the street. Crowds of people were moving about, shopping in whatever shops had not been looted. It was too early in the day for violence, which took time to smolder. Hugo waited — he would give the lad five minutes. Not that it mattered. He had nothing else to do. He was supposed to be negotiating with the fictitious Madach. Poor Ladislaus was counting on results. But no one could bring Bela back. Maybe Jeno could be rescued. Maybe some day, but not today. He would make it up to Jeno.

"Aren't you the priest who spoke in Dunauvaros?" The young man had returned with his older comrade.

"Yes."

"Would you do it again?" He was excited. "We heard about a priest with a limp who spoke like an orator."

So they marched again in the city. And Hugo limped along with them, up near the front. To hell with Fust. He had told Hugo to be a priest, so he would be a hell of a good one. Fust had always disappeared when Hugo needed him; there was something fishy about that.

The rebel leaders made many speeches, and Hugo said the same things he had said in Dunauvaros, promising them cities of gold and countryside of green and laughing people waving at a magnificent future. They were poetic people; they knew he did not mean it literally. That's why they had created a heaven — to supply a more perfect, literal happiness for afterward, because the heart craved it.

It was a week that stirred the world. Word went out on the airwaves how they chose freedom, defied Soviet might, endured atrocities. It was also a week of confusion, uncertainty about who was in control. At times they were the new Communists, at other times the new Catholic opposition; often the two seemed to be the same thing. New names kept turning up. Leaders made promises. Others, not doing so well, made confessions.

As the overwhelmingly Catholic population gained the upper hand for a while, the cry went up for Cardinal Brosky, a nationalist hero who had long been in jail. An army unit freed him in November, and he returned in triumph to his residence on a hill outside the city.

Then Fust was on the phone. Hugo couldn't decide whether to be glad or sorry — life was easier when Fust was presumed dead or at least out of circulation. He congratulated Hugo. "Your speeches improve all the time."

"Were you there?"

"Never mind."

"I had nothing to do with that killing in Dunauvaros."

"I know; I know. Neither had the others."

"Then why hold them?"

"Because the secret police are fools. But for now they're all we've got, and as you keep telling me the world is imperfect." Fust had a nimble mind. He might make a fascinating friend but that would have to be in another lifetime — Hugo blamed him for having ruined this one.

"I want you to do something with Brosky," Fust said. "Talk sense into him. He's the main symbol, and at times like this symbols are everything."

"Forget it. He's a cardinal: he wouldn't listen to a seminary teacher."

"We'll make it worth his while to listen." Talking to Fust, one always got the impression that everything was under control, or at least possible down the road if one simply had confidence enough to decide things were possible.

Two days later, Ladislaus and Hugo drove through the early morning. Brosky had agreed to see them. As they passed through the country villages there were lines of brooding Soviet tanks facing in various directions. It was not clear whether they were leaving or arriving. Soldiers' heads looked out from turrets. Two soldiers were roasted to death in their own iron tombs in Dunauvaros. Treacherous times.

"We should have brought the monsignor," Ladislaus said. He looked uncomfortable in a new suit without ashes on it.

"Relax. The monsignor is too old. He should be retired."

"You know he'd retire if the regime would give us a bishop."

"We'll see what the cardinal has to say about that."

Already in the early morning people were crowding the side street by Brosky's house, hoping for a look at him, a saint and legend.

A young priest admitted them. There was a musty smell in the house empty for so long. Ladislaus took out his pipe, replaced it again in his pocket. The young priest led them down a short corridor of red carpet to where the cardinal sat hunched by a fire with a rug on his knees. He was a gray, haggard man with a hangdog look. It was said Rome had chosen him because the country needed a martyr more than a scholar. He smiled wanly as they kissed his big episcopal ring.

"We're so glad Your Eminence is free," Ladislaus said.

"They tortured me in body and soul," he said.

Ladislaus told him about the uprising. He mentioned Bela, who had left the seminary and was killed.

"Brave lad," the cardinal said.

Ladislaus talked on about the affairs of the diocese, which was leaderless, he said. But when it was time to talk business, he looked at Hugo.

"Now that you're free, Cardinal, perhaps something can be done."

"I see nothing that can be done except to fight and suffer."

"Begging Your Eminence's pardon, there seems to be a more liberal regime on the way. They might be prepared to make concessions, allow some new bishops."

"In return for what?"

"If Your Eminence would just recognize the new regime." It was a gamble. Ladislaus had not intended any such bold request, but now that it was said he could not take it back. It was what Fust wanted; nothing less would do.

"I can't do that. It will still be a Communist regime."

"It will not be like before. They will give us religious freedom, support the schools, close the concentration camps, in return for official recognition."

"How do you know that?"

"Father Ovath has had much success negotiating with the regime," Ladislaus interjected. "If anyone can arrange it, he can."

"The Party wants peace and prosperity as much as we do," Hugo said. "And when the Soviets are gone things will be different."

"But they don't want God."

That was the rock against which so many Communist good intentions perished. Both sides could bargain and compromise about everything else, but either there was a God or there was not. If there was a God, the world was a different color. Everything hinged on it. The cardinal was looking inward for invisible grace more sought than found, while others were looking around them for smoking factories producing results less rarefied and more tangible for those prepared to settle for what seemed enough.

"Maybe in time, Your Eminence. We must make small beginnings."

"You don't know them. You have not faced their hate and torture."

Here Hugo had no good answer. He would pass along to Fust the superfluous information that hate and torture had certain disadvantages.

"If there were, let us say, some favorable gesture that Your Eminence could make..." Hugo had to take something back to Fust, some grain of success.

"They drove the sisters out of Beco. They would not let them teach." These did not seem world-class obstacles to peace. He was again the dogged peasant priest. "They tortured me until they broke me." That was more like a reason. Outside, the people were cheering him and calling his name, but he did not seem to hear them.

"No need to tell Madach that His Eminence is stubborn as a mule," Ladislaus said on the way home. "You could hold out some hope."

"Or we could petition Rome to have the cardinal replaced."

"God forgive you." Ladislaus was genuinely shocked until he concluded Hugo was joking, although Hugo had not been joking. Much as he loved Ladislaus, he would always be thinking a step or two ahead of him. It was essential to survival.

The promise of a new dawning was never fulfilled. The Soviet tanks turned around and crushed the people fighting with shovels and stones and bare fists. The world's outcry was a feeble whimper far away. Cardinal Brosky found refuge in the French embassy. New leaders ousted the old ones. Retaliation against enemies real or imagined was brutal and effective.

In the seminary recreation room there were new, soft chairs, and a television set had taken the place of the old radio. The presenter of the evening news was homegrown, with a local accent replacing the haughty BBC man of radio days. "As the Communist Party consolidates its power base, workers are happy to go back to work and students to go back to their classes...." No one jeered or mocked — that's how much things have changed, Hugo ruminated.

The disrupted class schedule was resumed. The students were again ready to listen to abstract theories about God and the metaphysical tricks that made the world go round however fitfully. There was no Bela to raise a challenging hand. Or to throw Jeno in Hugo's face.

And there was no Jeno to instigate protests. But there was hope that the new regime would close the camps. He would make it up to Jeno. Let him win every argument. Laugh heartily at every silly joke as they talked about old times.

On an occasional Sunday, after Mass, he would drive the long journey to the mountains to visit his parents. At the coming of winter he arrived with a beautiful new coat for his mother. It's so beautiful, she thought secretly, I could never wear it, not here in the mountains.

And back at the seminary, every night, while the others watched television or played cards, Hugo read books of every variety. He taught himself stilted versions of the more common foreign languages. He typed endless pages, looking for ways to figure things out, find a synthesis or any old thesis that would make everybody happy at the same time. Interrupted for a while by all the turmoil, he was back on track and would soon have two books ready for publication.

Chapter Sixteen

It was 1964. The years, which had dragged their feet when he was young, were rushing headlong as he grew older. He was thirty-nine. Approaching middle age — except that one could never be sure what was the middle, especially in a life as precarious as Hugo's.

In a new car, which he had pulled many strings to get, he drove in cheery sunshine listening to lively contemporary music on the radio.

In his pocket was a letter from his father, written in a rough angular hand. It said his mother was ill. It must be serious or he would not have written. Pang of regret for all the visits not made.

His destination was City Hall. High on the fifth floor Fust was installed in a mighty office, new minister of the interior. Now at last they could make things happen. Every year saw the weeks flash more swiftly before Hugo's eyes, ungraspable time flying away. There was an ever more desperate need to be aboard that hooting, impatient time train to some measurable destiny. Now Fust was chief engineer of that magic train.

"What have we here?" He was glad to see Hugo, who presented a brown paper bag.

"Open it. It's to celebrate."

"Champagne! You're a true priest." He found two chunky glasses in a closet and was excited pulling the cork with a pop. They clinked the glasses and laughed, and Fust slapped Hugo on the back, spilling champagne. He pulled up a chair beside Hugo by the window, which had a spectacular view looking down on a park.

"How does it feel to be important?" Hugo wished Fust could stay in this giddy, happy, indomitable, irrepressible mood forever — this was the Fust who had bought his soul when it was fresh and shining and worth something.

"Great. It feels great. I suppose I'm ambitious. Would you say I'm ambitious?"

"I would."

"That's honest at least."

"But you've done a good job."

"And so have you, Hugo. I consider you my greatest success."

"We're just getting started."

"You understand that at times I had to be tough, Hugo. Like that time..."

They looked soberly at each other.

"Say it — that time with Eva. Where is she, Zoltan?"

"You're better off not knowing." This time he stared Hugo down. "Besides, we have bigger things to talk about."

"Not to me, they're not bigger." A great difficulty in life was to know when exactly to take a stand. What disagreement was big enough to make it life-and-death? For Hugo it was a double dilemma. But Fust meanwhile had seized the moment. He pressed a button on his desk and a sleek young man entered.

"This is Imre Herzeg. He will be my right-hand man."

"Pleased to meet you," Hugo said. Imre's handshake was strong.

"An excellent job, Hugo." That meant he knew everything. Hugo wished Fust had consulted with him before letting the cat out of one more bag.

"Hugo's trip to Rome was very satisfactory," Fust now informed Imre. "The Vatican is eager for new bishops to fill several vacancies. Our immediate interest is in Hugo's friend, Ladislaus."

"Great," Imre said. Hugo disliked him. He smelled a rat.

"After that we will prime Ladislaus for cardinal."

Imre pointed at the gold watch on his wrist and backed out of the room with a vague wave. Hugo felt that in some ominous way this strange, steely little man had been inserted into his life without his having a chance to object.

"Did you see how thin his wrists are?" Fust was still trying to be merry. "Never trust a man with thin wrists." He laughed too heartily, perhaps from the champagne.

"What about Jeno?"

"Not now, Hugo."

"You promised me that when the camps were closed down, Jeno would be first man home."

"He was a difficult man, Hugo. People like that never change."

"He haunts my nights, Zoltan. I ask it as a personal favor — get him out."

The faded splendor of several centuries still clung to the cathedral of Dunauvaros. Statues of saints and angels came to life on this special day. Murals depicted Christianity at some of its finer turning points — for better or worse, the world would have been very different without it. The cathedral organ was played by a tall dark man from Belgium. Every inch of space was taken — the people saw this day as a portent of a new era. Even the Party had a representative prominent in a front pew, an unprecedented symbol of the new détente engineered by Fust and Hugo though implemented by others who took most of the credit.

Dozens of priests and bishops entered in procession, along with other ministers bearing thurible, cross, lectionary — and at the back the subdued figure of Ladislaus in gold vestments used by other bishops for nearly a thousand years. He had grown more sallow, his face creased and craggy.

A cardinal from Rome presided at the consecration of Ladislaus as bishop of Dunauvaros. At the end the choir sang "Ecce Sacerdos Magnus" — behold the great priest.

A year later, Bishop Ladislaus had appointed Hugo director of the seminary. He sat at the head table and tinkled the bell that regulated the students' lives. When fall came he limped around the front lawn to meet the new novices and helped them carry their cases upstairs as Ladislaus had once done.

"Benedicamus Domino," he said in the refectory.

"Deo Gratias," they answered.

But when the formalities were over Hugo did not know what to say to those in his charge. So he said what Ladislaus had said, not believing it, but not knowing it was wrong either.

It was, besides, a heady time to be Catholic. In 1964 Ladislaus had slipped away quietly to Rome to join thousands of other bishops at the epochal Second Vatican Council.

"Only a score of them in twenty centuries," Hugo said. "Most of them have been turning points in the history of Christianity." He walked with the seminarians after dinner the way Ladislaus used to do. It was fall again, the days getting shorter. Squirrels were busy collecting nuts under majestic trees. They were smarter than people at providing for the future.

The jolly Pope John XXIII had surprised the world by calling for a council to let in fresh air, Hugo said, to the cobwebby upper echelons of the church.

"Not reform, renewal," one new student corrected another.

"It's not a perfect church, then?" a shaggy student asked. The years came and went, but the students just recycled themselves in conformity with basic human nature. The shaggy student's name was Ambrose, a cross between Jeno and Antal, with a few attributes of his own mixed in. He was playing the haughty upstart but with the legendary heart of gold for moral ballast.

"It was damn nearly perfect until you arrived," another student answered.

The pope invited theologians and dignitaries and observers as well as the bishops. He wanted the whole human race to have a hand in creating a new church if possible. They debated about faith and morals and worship. They dusted off neglected old concepts and found them to be fascinating and reminiscent of how pure was the alleged message of Jesus Christ and how people back then placed greater emphasis on loving each other, and even their enemies, than on making rules or observing them.

Not that it was all smooth sailing. The human church was ruled by crusty old men who had long grown accustomed to having things their way. Some were holy as well as crusty, but sometimes it took centuries to tell who was smart and who was holy and who merely crusty when God insisted on keeping his hands in his pockets and his head in the clouds.

The ebb and flow of council debates spread like cool — and sometimes hot — breezes around the world. They seeped into seminaries, including Dunauvaros.

"Will they change the law on celibacy?" Ambrose asked.

"Probably not."

"It's a ridiculous law."

The more things stayed the same, Hugo thought, the more magnified were the differences. Bela wanted to die for the cause, as did Jeno before that. They sought nothing for themselves. The cause was country or faith or freedom, something big and far away and vague enough never to be totally achieved; that was the beauty of it. Ambrose was getting closer to home. It was harder for anyone fighting over celibacy to die a hero.

On the other hand, who said everyone had to be a hero? Maybe it was enough just to get by. Maybe encourage the down and out at the bottom of life's pit. Neither church nor Party did enough of that, Hugo reflected. He resolved to write about it. About everything. Wanting clarity.

And sometimes when he saw students lost in prayer in the chapel, Hugo envied them. If he could pull off that unique feat of praying, he would be almost that perfect priest he had promised to be. But he had never promised as much to God as he did to Fust.

Chapter Seventeen

Once she had asked him to climb the hill at the back of the house to get holly because it was the day before Christmas. She gave him a knife from the kitchen drawer and said to be sure there were berries on the holly. The first snow of winter was falling, and he wanted to play with Ferenc, but he went because it was his mother. The berries were all near the top, and he climbed to dangerous heights. When he looked down she was there watching, in her brown coat, saying come down or you'll kill yourself. He vowed that day that he'd buy her a fur coat, a vow it took too long to keep. How was he to know that his life would get derailed?

Driving toward the mountains Hugo feared she would be dead before he arrived. He felt the same heaviness as on the day he left home for the seminary. There was little in life as sad as departures. He rounded a bend and could see blue smoke rising from the stone chimney into the balmy air.

"I was worried you wouldn't make it." His father was wearing a tie and his Sunday suit. Behind him in the doorway loomed Ferenc, who squeezed Hugo's hand in great earnestness. His face was thin and pinched. Neighbors and relatives filled the big kitchen.

It was the first time he had ever seen her in bed, always first up in the morning and last to bed at night. She was propped on pillows. He kissed her tired face, took her hand, a withered hand like an old leaf.

"How do you feel?"

"Not so good."

"Any pain?"

"It could be worse." Her voice was weak; she would not last long. "I'm glad you're here."

"And did the priest come?"

"Yes, he has been very good." The dark priest who had once beaten

Hugo was now the parish priest, old but resolute, still cycling the mountain roads but more often walking beside the bicycle. "He says you will be a bishop."

"And if I am, you'll be in the front row when I get the pointy hat."

"I'll be there in spirit."

"Do you remember the Christmas you sent me out for holly, with the kitchen knife, and it was snowing, and you came out in your brown coat in case anything had gone wrong?"

"I remember all the Christmases," she said, but he could see that she did not remember that particular one. She was tired; her eyes were closing. He joined the others in the kitchen.

"Did you hear I'm back." Ferenc cornered him. "Out of the Party," he added to clarify.

"Yes, I'm delighted, Ferenc."

"God is good."

"Did the Party give you any trouble?"

"None whatever." That meant he was of no use to them in the first place. Unless. A shiver went up Hugo's back. No — they would never try it twice. And not twice from the same family. And not without telling Hugo. But they were notoriously bad at telling. And notoriously unpredictable. It was disturbing. He would observe Ferenc and talk to him later in search of further clues.

Later, everybody was called to the bedroom while he gave her the sacrament of the sick, extreme unction, praying in a low voice that God's angels would greet her at the wide gate of Paradise, and more than ever in his life he wanted it to be true. A sort of brightness came to her, as if all the cares that pounded life to death were put in perspective for her at last, the body being rolled back and time and eternity falling into focus.

They buried her in a graveyard surrounded by tall trees. They knelt by the open grave, and the dark priest knelt beside Hugo, who asked God to take her spirit to vertiginous heights among the stars and make her young again and laughing on a soft heavenly seat and waited upon by saints and angels vying with each other for her company. He asked for some glimmer that would light his own life, challenging God to point the way if indeed there was a way and if indeed there was a God.

✠

A lone boat with white sails passed slowly down the lake. On a wooden deck down the hill from the country club Fust and Hugo sat at a rustic table with drinks. Hugo's casual dress had gradually become more sophisticated; he could pass for a man of the world, not like the average priest who looked like a fish out of water in anything but the long soutane and back-to-front white collar. Fust was leaning back and listening more attentively than usual, while Hugo talked quietly but urgently.

"And I wanted so badly to tell her. She was dying — it was not as if she was going to tell anyone. She was rounding out her life, making things tidy. But I was the great loose end, and she didn't even know, or at least I think she didn't know.

"Sure, I knew it would break her heart. But at least I wouldn't be sending her off thinking I was someone I am not. But I couldn't tell her, Zoltan. And she died not knowing who the hell I really am — me, her son, Zoltan." He paused and fought back tears. Seagulls swooped over the water and complained to one another. Fust said nothing, unusually reflective, taking an occasional sip from his drink.

"So, suddenly, it became very important to me — whether there is life, or whatever, afterward — you know? So I went to Ladislaus — no, no need to panic, I didn't spill the beans. I thought I could somehow pin down Ladislaus about whether there is a future afterward and all that. Stupid of me, really. On that question, everyone is alone. You have to make your own blind leap, one way or another. Don't look in books, Ladislaus said. It is through the knees that grace enters, he said, not through the head. At that moment I envied the old bastard and wished I were like him."

He paused and sighed. "And I concluded I had failed both Ladislaus and you, by not being the best priest in the whole goddamn world — which begins on your knees."

Chapter Eighteen

The 747 circled Rome as if searching for the airport. Fust had the window seat, and Hugo stretched across him in search of famous monuments.

"You're acting like a peasant, Hugo," Fust said.

"I am a peasant, Zoltan. I had hoped to see St. Peter's or at least the Colosseum, but all I can see is a soccer stadium."

"Take a good look at that stadium, my boy. In years to come it will be more famous than the others, site of the 1960 Olympics. Surely you agree that pleasure has already put religion in the shade."

Beautiful young girls were collecting the lunch trays. Pleasure was making a strong bid for people's loyalty — Hugo could not deny it.

On the aisle seat sat the smug Imre. He was a new breed rising in the Party, not a wing-it pioneering Communist like Fust but a bureaucrat. He carried the papers in his leather briefcase, kept track of details and schedules. However, Hugo noted soberly, when decisions needed to be made the kind of information Imre had stored away in his head and briefcase gave him a lot of power.

They were met by Monsignor Conlon, a big, well-fed, extroverted man with booming voice, ostentatious with red trim on his long robes. It was disappointing to be met by an American in this legendary city, but a stark reminder of how universal the church was.

"Welcome to the Holy City," Conlon said. "His Eminence regrets that he could not be here to meet you." Hugo had been studying Italian. He guessed the American's accent was a travesty of the real thing. From the limousine Conlon pointed out historical landmarks, including the Colosseum and eventually St. Peter's.

In an elegant Vatican dining room, that evening, there was dinner for five.

"Everyone says I'm the one who looks like an Italian, and Cardinal Pogioli here looks more like a German." Conlon was in full voice. "I think the cardinal spent too many years abroad as a Vatican diplomat. He missed out on the spaghetti."

"You should try this liqueur," the small, suave Pogioli said. "It's made by the Servite Brothers at their monastery in Monte Senario. I find it to be excellent."

Everything they cast their eyes or hands on seemed burdened by history. The table at which they sat had been used by fourteen popes, Conlon said. Even Imre seemed impressed. Since no one else mentioned him, the rambunctious Fust, able to hold out no longer, asked if the pope was in town, and where his apartments were, and if the cardinal would convey Fust's felicitations, yes and those of everyone else back home. The cardinal said he would but did not promise an audience with His Holiness, which for Fust, in his present mood, would be some kind of small crowning achievement and might even cause him to return to the church — Hugo liked Fust best when he was like this.

He was grateful for this opportunity to talk with them, Cardinal Pogioli said. He hoped their visit would mark the beginning of a new understanding. He talked on quietly in generalities. Eventually specifics had to be mentioned.

"Our great wish is the reinstatement of Cardinal Brosky," Pogioli said.

"That is unacceptable," Imre jumped in. Pogioli looked at him in surprise, and Fust scorched him with a look of his own. That was Imre's only contribution to the evening.

"We too are eager to have the cardinal reinstated in his see," Fust stepped in, "but this man is ill."

"The Catholics of your country need a leader," Pogioli said. "They have been deprived already too long."

"Perhaps someone else could be found?" Fust raised a questioning eyebrow.

"The people would feel betrayed — you know what they think of Brosky."

Fust looked at Hugo, his cue to take over.

"Perhaps a first small step could be made," Hugo said. "If His Holiness could appoint another cardinal, stationed here in Rome for the present, it would be a great honor for our people. Mr. Fust assures us the government would not be opposed. Then, after the Brosky dilemma is solved, the new man could return to his homeland."

"Very interesting" — Pogioli, by Vatican standards, practically threw caution to the wind. "I am not in a position to respond to your suggestion, Father Ovath, but it is, well — very interesting."

When it was time to give diplomacy a rest, the affable Conlon took over again. He knew everything about wine. He told them bland jokes in English that Hugo then had to translate for Imre. But Hugo was convinced that the clerical blarney hid a steely center and what the Americans liked to call a can-do personality. In weeks to come American cardinals and other heavyweights would learn about this visit. His own name would be mentioned. The world was wide. He resolved to work harder at getting to know it.

"There is one more area about which we are concerned," Pogioli said at the end of the evening. "We were pleased by the release of so many political and religious prisoners by your government, but there are still several of our priests in captivity. Their release would be a great advance in our ongoing good relations."

"I will mention it to the prime minister," Fust said. "But I must remind you that those still held were those obstinately outspoken against our government. Still, I will see what can be done."

In the seminary recreation room, a dozen students were in high spirits, drinking cans of beer until the announcer on the television reached the cause of their excitement. "And today comes word from the Vatican that Bishop Ladislaus Cernos of Dunauvaros has been elevated to the rank of cardinal." Ladislaus then appeared on the screen, arm out greeting someone. "The new cardinal will be moving to Rome, sources say, to work for the church's central curia."

The raucous students applauded. Two students arranged their plastic collars askew and imitated Ladislaus's handshake. On the television Ladislaus was being interviewed.

"I don't even speak the language," he was saying.

"Not to worry, bishop," the jokey interviewer said. "They say that knowledge of wine is the shortest road to power in Rome."

"I'm sorry to say I have little interest in power either. I'm afraid they picked the wrong man for the job."

He went back to greeting well-wishers on a street in the city.

He cut a benevolent swath through life shaking hands and wishing people well.

The whole world seemed to gather momentum. Pools that were long stagnant grew new lilies. The stony soil that the new regime had worked so hard to cultivate was sending up sprouts. The special field that Fust and Hugo had plowed and tilled looked green and promising. Peace, however shaky, was chasing prosperity. Optimism raised its head and smiled at people on the street. Church and state were shaking hands and again on speaking terms, even if they did not always speak the same language. The recent Vatican Council in Rome had prompted the church to shed years of stagnation and open up to new thinking and risk rubbing shoulders with the real world. Possibilities seemed endless.

It was 1969. At forty-four Hugo was appointed bishop of Dunauvaros to fill the vacancy left by Ladislaus. It was no great surprise. His books were in all the bookstores. He was interviewed by journalists when something new happened. His hair, now quite gray, was still unruly as in his youth, but, slyly cultivated, this gave him the aura of a bohemian prelate who ought not to be lumped with his often rustic colleagues.

The crowds flocking to attend his ordination as bishop were greater than those that, several years earlier, had come to pay homage to Ladislaus. Thousands stood outside in the rain. They came because he had fought on their side in 1957, and before that at Berkos, had even gone to jail for them. He was larger than life. Ladislaus was the presiding prelate. After all the bishops had placed their hands on Hugo's head willing the Holy Spirit to come down from heaven, Ladislaus climbed into the high pulpit, carved in the shape of an eagle. He preached about Hugo being consecrated bishop in order to lift people up. Hugo remembered that once, at summer camp, an officer with a straight back and a flat haircut had exhorted the young men to lift the world up. But the Party did not venture to raise its sights as high: only to the horizon. The church dared to look up however blinkingly into the sun. Hugo resolved vaguely to try to do what a bishop should do. He would help the Party take the people as high as the horizon. But on good days he would urge them higher, kicking their asses in the hope that they might take the great leap beyond. There was nothing ideologically wrong with that, he figured.

There was a reception afterward. Ladislaus was on Hugo's right. His black pipe was perched in a saucer.

"I have good news," he said. "I've been keeping it up my sleeve as a present. Jeno is coming home."

"What — coming home!"

"In a week or so. I have arranged for him to stay at the seminary."

"That's fantastic news." It would again be like the old days. Jeno would be joking and doing stupid things to embarrass people. Hugo would be his bishop and boss — what a laugh that would be for Jeno, who would give Hugo hell, but he would love it. He would invite Jeno to the bishop's residence for a week. Fatten him up. Relive old times. What Hugo did not tell Ladislaus was that he had known for some time about Jeno's upcoming release.

"What about Bishop Illyes?" It had always seemed risky to ask about Illyes. No one ever mentioned him, as if the subject were taboo — some code of silence was at work all those years that baffled Hugo.

"We have no word about him," Ladislaus said.

"Was he really such a rebel?"

"I was young myself at that time, so most of what I know is hearsay. Illyes had a problem. The bottle."

"But they didn't throw him in jail just for having a drinking problem?"

"No. Nothing is ever as simple as it seems, Hugo. You know his picture on the wall at the seminary? Well, he looks like a timid little man. But he went on defying the regime. He had an arsenal of guns and stuff like that at the palace, to supply the freedom-fighters. Some said he was like that only when he was drinking. I don't know."

"What happened to him?"

"His disappearance remains a mystery to this day. You know how hard it is to get the facts after they take someone — we've had the same problem getting information on Jeno. But the story is, Illyes made a confession. It may not have been his fault. Without the drink, his courage would have left him. Hard to say. And it's so long ago — he could be dead now."

People came up to the head table to shake Hugo's hand, interrupting the conversation. He was a popular choice for bishop. They wanted leadership. Miklos and Antal came by, especially proud. Life had smoothed Antal's wide variety of rough edges. Miklos had become a recluse and was writing musical Masses that required more choir members and orchestral muscle than the diocese of Dunauvaros was likely ever to muster.

"Remember your classmates," Antal said. "Blood is thicker than water."

"Some wanted to take down the Illyes picture at the seminary," Ladislaus said when the others had gone. "But no decision was made, and talk about him soon died down. I suppose he was an embarrassment."

"Don't worry: that picture won't be taken down in my time," Hugo assured him.

Hugo parked by the stone wall outside the old railway station, scene of so many comings and goings. He could never walk through those doors without thinking of his mother. But now he was buoyant: he would surprise Jeno. The waiting people were festive. The train would be bringing tourists from eastern cities and family members coming home on vacation. An elderly woman in black stood looking into that speck of distance where the train would appear. Like a figure in a Greek tragedy: she represented the less luminous reality. Prisoners were trickling back from the camps to pick up the remains of their lives. The train was ten minutes late.

When it seemed the train had disgorged its last passenger, Jeno appeared. Hugo hid behind a pillar to surprise him. Jeno stood looking back into the train. Then he came slowly forward. Looking puzzled. He carried a canvas bag cradled in his arms. He looked gaunt, his face white and pasty. He looked around at people greeting friends and family, unsure what to do.

Hugo stepped forward, placing himself in front of Jeno, and grinned wide enough to span the years. But it was long moments before recognition sparked in Jeno's eyes. Hugo held out his arms and they embraced. Hugo embraced the old Jeno he once knew, not sure if this were the same Jeno in his arms.

"Welcome home, Jeno."

"You have red buttons, Hugo." He was puzzled. There was a hint of disapproval. It was the kind of joke he himself might have played if the tables were turned, dressing up like a bishop, although he would probably have done it with more panache, high hat and all, Hugo thought. Jeno looked back again at the train.

"Are you with someone, Jeno?"

"Not me."

"Here, give me the bag. It's so good to see you, you old rascal."

Jeno released the bag reluctantly. "It's good to see you too, Hugo." He was wearing an old blue suit that did not fit. "Does Ladislaus know I'm out?"

"Ladislaus was sorry he couldn't be here to greet you himself. He's a cardinal now."

"A cardinal? Who's going to run the seminary?"

"Don't worry. We'll find somebody."

"That's a lovely car, Hugo. It's very shiny."

"I washed it specially for you, Jeno. I wanted to impress you — I swear to God." Hugo held the door, and Jeno cautiously sat in the passenger seat.

He would kill Fust for this. For not telling him. For not warning him. As Hugo drove through the town, Jeno worried that they would have an accident, looking in all directions and making faces. It was useless to kill Fust. He knew what Fust would say. Fust didn't do it. What difference if Fust had told him that Jeno had, along the way, lost his mind? If he had known Jeno was bonkers, would he still have gone down to the station to meet him? Would he have gone alone or taken someone with him to lighten the load of guilt and help make conversation with this poor wretch waiting any minute to be killed in a car crash after all he had survived in the camps?

"You have red buttons," Jeno said again in the seminary dining room, eating dinner with Antal and Hugo. He ate with great urgency. Hugo poured wine, which Jeno drank down like water.

"That's because Hugo is a bishop now," Antal explained. "There have been a lot of changes while you were away. But don't worry, we'll soon bring you up to scratch."

"A bishop? You'll make a good bishop, Hugo."

"Thanks, Jeno. I'll need your help."

"Anything you want, Hugo. We were always good friends, weren't we, Hugo?" After Jeno filled another glass, Hugo quietly removed the wine bottles.

"Do you remember the day you put on Ladislaus's soutane and came out smoking his pipe?"

"I never did that," he said defensively.

"Yes, you did. You had your arms gesticulating the way Ladislaus does; everyone was laughing." Please, Jeno, let it be a joke — that was Hugo's last slender hope: that Jeno might be pulling off the best caper of his life, one of the great practical jokes of all time.

"What was it like, Jeno?" Antal asked. "In the camp?"

"Oh it was very nice; you'd be surprised." He looked over his shoulder. "We did a lot of work."

"What kind of work?"

"I have a gift for my mother. Do you think they'll mind?"

"No one will mind, Jeno," Hugo assured him. "What did you bring her?"

He had insisted on keeping the canvas bag at his feet. Now he retrieved it and searched until he found a brown paper package. He opened it awkwardly but carefully. It was a cheese sandwich of black bread, bruised and revolting after its long journey from the camps. He looked at Hugo eagerly for approval.

"Put it away carefully for now, Jeno. Your mother will be delighted to see you."

"Did they ever punish you?" Antal asked.

"It was for our own good, Antal. It was a way of reminding us. There has to be order, Antal, or you get nothing done."

"That's all history now, Jeno," Antal said. "You're not going back there and that's all."

"I don't mind — whatever you say, Antal."

"And guess what. We're putting you back in your old room on the second floor. Only you'll sleep better because Hugo won't be next door and snoring."

"I don't mind — Hugo is my friend." He cradled the canvas bag. His walk was slow. Whatever they did to him, more than his mind was damaged.

Chapter Nineteen

The bishop's residence was modest by episcopal standards, a yellow house surrounded by old drooping trees. The best room, Hugo had been happy to discover, was the study, considerably bigger than what he was used to. With the latest in typewriters, copiers, and other appliances, subsidized by the Party, he had turned it into an efficient machine for thinking, writing, and scheming.

"There is a person to see you in the parlor," the housekeeper said after a discreet knock. When she left the gender vague, Hugo knew it was a woman — whenever it was a man she called him a man.

He slipped his plastic collar into place and slipped into his black jacket as he went. He knew before she turned around.

Her misty smile had not faded. Twenty-five years rolled back. He was a bishop now; that was his own first thought. He could think of nothing suitable to say. Besides, it was her move: she had caught him at a disadvantage, without an appointment, no time to brace himself. He stretched out his hand, kept it at a distance as they shook.

"I suppose I should have made an appointment."

"Not you, Eva. There was no need."

The misty smile was there, but the years could not be denied. She was a woman going through middle age, heavier. The makeup did not hide the lines around her eyes. A colorful scarf added a vague touch of class. As if she needed it.

"Are you surprised? You look surprised."

"Yes, I suppose I am." They stood inspecting each other, checking the damage done by the years. "It's warmer in my study. Give me your coat." It was a fur coat and looked expensive.

"I suppose I should call you bishop."

"It's not funny."

"I know."

They were awkward and a bit embarrassed as he flustered to tidy a space in the office and clear papers and his breviary from a chair. They were to have shared a little house by a stream while they raised children a few miles outside some perfect village in some perfect world. He offered her a drink and she declined. He suggested coffee and she nodded, the eyes misty. He went to tell the housekeeper. Eva was scanning the study as he returned. So this, she must be thinking, is what became of him. He did not know her well enough, then or ever, to be able to say if she might be impressed. Their ships had indeed passed rather swiftly in the night.

"How did you know where to find me?"

"You must be joking. You're famous, Hugo."

The coffee arrived. The housekeeper looked severe and disapproving. She left the door just a little bit ajar. Hugo closed it with a bang.

"I suppose you're wondering why I called."

"Yes, a little."

"Unfinished business, I guess. I felt I owed you an explanation. Something like that. Each year I made a resolution to do it, but the year would pass. And now that the political climate has grown — how shall I say? — more benign, here I am."

"What happened, Eva?"

"They gave me a terrible choice — my son or you."

"And you took your son?" All Hugo was being asked to give up was Fust, he reflected bitterly. The odds had not been even.

"Sorry, Hugo." She took a photo from her bag and handed it to Hugo. The typical mother. "He's a man now. He works for the government." She was proud of him. And indeed he was a strapping fellow who looked like her, standing beside a motorcycle. "His name is Arthur. Doesn't it sound British?"

"And yourself?"

"What about me?"

"For example, did you marry?" Her hair looked so beautiful and brown, no trace of gray, he guessed it was dyed, at least a little.

"No."

It was too late. Not because he was a bishop. Not because they were too old. But because, one day, without his even noticing it, the love for her died inside him, gradually evaporated, unable ever to be snared again out of the capricious air.

"May I call to see you again?"

"It's better not to."

"Please, Hugo. Life is so short and the world so harsh, we should do all we can to ease the pain."

"Short, Eva, and very complicated."

She stood and put the coffee cup down on his desk. The visit was winding down. "It's not that I'm asking for anything — please don't misunderstand, Hugo. All that was long ago." She stood gazing at him until he went and got her coat and held it for her. Twenty-five years might fall away if he just put his arms around her; that was how complicated life was. "You're not angry at me?"

He opened the study door for her, then the front door. He took both her hands in his hands. Sturdy little bony hands. "I promise — every time I see the moon for the rest of my life, I will think of you. And I won't think of anyone else, only you."

Their hands squeezed and parted. He stood in the doorway until the car eased away, remembering how once she had closed the door behind him to keep out the pain.

Every time there was an unexpected turn in Hugo's life, the old fear would stab at him. What now? What if? His two lives were so entangled and yet at cross-purposes, it was a miracle that no stray suspicion had escaped through the chinks of carelessness or routine. The frisson ran up his spine again when a telegram arrived from Ladislaus. He would be arriving on Monday. Very sudden, and no explanation. If his world were to come tumbling down burying him, he would never have expected Ladislaus to be the cause of his downfall. His imagination grew wings as he waited at the airport.

It was 1976.

It was no longer possible for Hugo to be anonymous, betrayed by his limp and his face familiar from television and the newspapers. So he was invited to wait in the VIP lounge. He sat in an armchair by a wall of glass and watched the planes arriving and leaving. Many were from the West: BOAC, TWA, Alitalia. Faces were dwarfed inside the little windows. They walked through the lounge so preoccupied. Perhaps important. Occasionally beautiful. Citizens of the mysterious other world where democracy meant something else entirely. More free-wheeling. There were so many ways the world could be run, but no perfect way. Many came through with briefcases, coming to do business. The regime was allowing that other world to filter in and show its wares.

Eventually Ladislaus came pushing through an entrance. He was wearing none of the red that cardinals like to wear. He peered around until he saw Hugo. He waved, then came forward eagerly, his hand out.

"Welcome, Ladislaus. None of that old Roman kissing for us, eh?"

A limousine with a chauffeur waited at the door. Ladislaus looked puzzled and suspicious. The government was merely showing its appreciation and respect, Hugo said with a flourish. This kind of cooperation was common in the West where church and state had ironed out their differences. "Your friend Madach insisted," he said as he held the door for Ladislaus.

For a while Ladislaus talked to the chauffeur, asking about his family. Then he dozed. It was disquieting. It was July and the smell of fresh-cut grass came through the open window. A farmer lifted his straining back and waved his hat. Every chance he got, Hugo spoke in favor of leaving their fields to the little farmers. He would mention Berkos, now a thriving community, where incidentally they had erected a statue in his honor. The farmer knew the four corners of his little field and where water lodged in winter and on which sunny bank in summer an odd flower grew — his land could not surprise or betray him. Sure, Hugo knew that was only half the story, the poetic half, and that there were hardship and heartbreak too. It didn't matter that no one could name it — he knew in his bones that something irrevocable would be lost if the little farms were turned into food factories. "There's the tower." Ladislaus woke up. Between the trees they could see the seminary. "I'm afraid I dozed, Hugo. Forgive me. I didn't sleep a wink last night. I was afraid the plane would come down in the mountains."

The housekeeper laid on a fine gastronomical performance, and Ladislaus had brought a bottle of wine from Rome, though when Hugo read the fine print he discovered it was from California.

"I suppose you're wondering why I'm here," Ladislaus finally said.

"You're damn right I am. You sounded very mysterious."

"What you probably don't realize, Hugo, is the great impact you have made abroad." He had come downstairs wearing an American T-shirt advertising lawnmowers, and Hugo had accused him of corruption at the hands of Monsignor Conlon. "Détente is what everybody is talking about, Hugo. They love that word in Rome. And not surprisingly you get the credit for starting détente between church and Party here at home. And now it is spreading. The Communists seem to be realizing that you can't stuff God into a box and bury him." He wiped his face with a napkin.

"If there's a compliment hidden there somewhere, I do appreciate it."

"More than a compliment. His Holiness wants to make you a cardinal."

"Don't make jokes, Ladislaus." He knew immediately it was a weak response. He was rattled; there was no denying it. Yes, it had crossed his mind that something like this could happen, but he had never considered the real-life baggage that came with the idea. Sure, Fust would have a rare orgasm. More success than even Fust had bargained for. And Hugo would walk through St. Peter's dressed in ermine under the eyes of the world, already making history, other princes of the church from far away countries traipsing by his side.

"It would mean moving to Rome," Ladislaus said.

"And you moving back here, now that Brosky's dead? I knew you had something to do with this, you old conniver."

"I didn't speak against it; that is all I'll say." He held up his glass of red California wine. The glasses clinked, a harmonious sound. Blue smoke from his pipe hung suspended under the lamp in the corner. He would go on smoking heartily as death came up the road to meet him, undismayed by an enigmatic God waiting to ask questions.

"When can I see Jeno?" he asked.

"Any time. You'll find him sitting out there at the seminary under a tree."

Exuberant Hugo drove at high speed to the city. This time the secret was his, and Fust, the maestro of one-upmanship, was in the dark. The bottle of champagne, their usual mode of celebration, was in a brown bag on the car floor. He admired the scenery. He admired the children going to school. He admired everything, even the new factories and blocks of apartments springing up wherever a few roads intersected. Soon the planners would learn style, maybe pick up aesthetic tips abroad, and humanize those massive chunks of concrete — Rome wasn't built in a day.

The July day turned sour as soon as he reached the parking lot. Heavy equipment threatened to crush his car. No parking space, he was told; major renovations were under way. He would not stoop to telling them he was a cardinal, or almost. He found a side street.

In the vestibule, under the great dome, he found the same feverish demolition and renovation. There was no uniformed attendant to either help or hinder him, so he climbed the formidable stairs, clutching the brown bag.

He knocked on Fust's door. There was no answer. He pushed open the door. The office was bare, stripped of all furnishings.

"Zoltan! Anyone home? Hey!" There was a phone on the floor and scattered papers, and Lenin's picture was still on the wall. Fust appeared in the doorway. He looked dazed. "What the hell is going on?" Hugo asked.

"Changes — that's what's going on."

"I brought champagne. Let's go someplace and celebrate."

"Imre is waiting for us." All the energy and confidence had deserted Fust.

"I'm sorry about your wife, Zoltan." She had died since Hugo last saw him. All he said was, "Imre is waiting."

"Forget Imre."

Fust, the survivor, grabbed Hugo by the collar and shook him. "Now listen to me. Do you want to get killed?" He did not wait for an answer. "Then watch your step." He stuck his face close to Hugo's, driving home the message. He turned and Hugo followed him down the corridor. A plaque on the door read "Imre Herzeg."

The office reminded Hugo of the botanical gardens: it was overwhelmed from floor to ceiling with flowers and plants. Imre, behind his ultramodern steel desk, did not look up.

"Sit down, gentlemen," he said.

"I've handed your dossier over to Imre." Fust tried to explain away the calamity that had fallen on him.

"What Zoltan means is, we're reevaluating. The thing is, Hugo, this venture may have been a mistake." He finally looked up. He was a master of the studied gesture.

"What are you talking about?"

"All the advantage has been to your church."

"It's not my church."

"Please!" He was so young. Not yet thirty, Hugo figured. He had spent two years in Leningrad, at some management school. "Don't get hysterical, Father Ovath," he was saying. "We gave your church freedom of religion. We gave them bishops. Even a cardinal. And now they want another."

"And this time it's me."

"Is it?"

"You would stop me becoming cardinal?"

"I wouldn't say it like that."

Hugo jumped up and turned on Fust, sitting mute in his chair. "What is going on here?"

"Sit down at once," Imre commanded, now on his feet too.

"You stupid little upstart," Hugo shouted. He picked up the chair he had been sitting on, brought it down with all his might, barely missing Imre, who must have learned a few physical moves in Leningrad. The chair smashed into pieces on his desk. A handgun had meanwhile miraculously appeared in Imre's hand and was now leveled at Hugo, who looked at Fust in consternation.

"We can't let him, Zoltan. We've come so far. He can't kill us both."

Each face registered its own tension and calculation. Everything hinged on Fust. Who decided not to be a hero. "Please, Hugo, the decision is made."

"Thanks, Zoltan," Imre sounded genuinely grateful. "Get Father Ovath another chair." He knew how to get under Hugo's skin. Fust obediently got another chair for Hugo. Imre put the gun in his belt like a hoodlum. He postured a little with it, like a cowboy, grinning at Hugo. He picked up a miniature green can and proceeded to water the plants, even turning his back on the others. For a moment Hugo felt admiration for his courage, until he concluded that Imre had some strategy up his sleeve.

"There you are, babies," Imre said to the plants. "Here's what you'll do, Hugo," he went on. "You call a press conference and announce that you are leaving the church. It's a matter of conscience. You just don't believe that stuff anymore."

"I'm sorry for the outburst." Hugo decided to try humility. "But the Party has benefited from détente as well as the church."

"Tell me how."

"Peace, for one thing. If concessions were not made they would have revolted again and again. You don't understand them, Imre."

"Revolt we can deal with."

"You mean, by force?"

"Of course."

"You can't shoot them all."

"No need to shoot them all, just a certain number. They understand decisiveness."

"Yes, especially the dead ones." Hugo tried talking quietly like Imre, no more broken chairs. "You don't understand what the most ignorant peasant knows in his heart. Their God is a trickier God than a dumb shit like you could ever imagine."

"And then — are you following me? — and then you say you are joining the Party. A matter of conscience. They're big on conscience — you know that." He liked his own nimble way with words. He had climbed to power on a wave of words over the carcass of Fust and others who had done the work. It was useless to argue. He was looking for some kind of measurable success. One could not measure peace, or even prosperity, and least of all happiness. He was a true materialist, Hugo realized, a rare thing even in a Communist.

"I won't do it."

"I understand it's a bit sudden." Imre put down the watering can. He looked at his watch. "Perhaps in a day or two you'll see it more clearly. Let's say, Thursday." Without warning he took the gun from his belt, aimed it at a clay pot hanging from the ceiling, blew the pot to smithereens. He carelessly threw the gun back in his desk drawer. He did not look at the two as he dismissed them.

"See him out, Zoltan," he said.

The pathetic bottle of champagne was on the floor by Imre's desk. Fust picked it up and handed it to Hugo.

"Some other time."

He used to row this lake on August days of seminary vacation. The mountain still looked down at its reflection in the water. Boulders clung to the sides and threatened to come tumbling down and cause havoc. Water birds still rose out of the reeds, complaining hoarsely, their webbed feet sticking out behind. There were unaccountable streaks of agitation across the water, the rest of it sheer as glass.

"Step in, Jeno." Hugo stood on a rock and held the boat steady.

"Are you sure it won't sink?" He was still hugging his old canvas bag; he took it everywhere.

"No danger."

Seven years out of the camp, Jeno had put on weight and looked bronzed and healthy. He spent his days in vague unawareness walking around the seminary grounds.

For several summers Hugo had planned this trip, just he and Jeno on the lake like old times. This was Tuesday. There might not be another chance. Thursday was Imre's deadline.

Hugo rowed at a leisurely pace. Whether mighty ocean or trickling brook, something soothing was carried by water from the heart of the earth to thirsting soul and aching body. Jeno ran his hand through it and said it was cold. The blue boat belonged to the diocese, as did a cabin in the trees. "Do you think this is the same blue boat?"

Jeno did not seem to hear. Hugo recalled Ladislaus sitting in the stern on an evening that rained, a towel on his head, urging four theology students to row like hell.

"It's beautiful as ever, Jeno."

"It is."

"Do you remember the day we got caught in a thunderstorm, and you splashed Ladislaus with your oar?"

"It must have been someone else, Hugo. I wouldn't splash Ladislaus."

"It was only a joke, Jeno." Beautiful swans swam in a regal procession, going in the opposite direction, their reflections upside down, occasionally sticking their long necks in the water to see what was happening below. The water made a constant slapping sound against the bottom of the boat.

"That day they took you away, Jeno — what did they say?"

"They said there were complaints about me. But I wasn't dangerous, Hugo. All I wanted was to overthrow the government."

"Did they hurt you?"

"They had to do it, Hugo. It wasn't their fault."

"Did they say who complained about you?"

"No, they never said, Hugo. I asked them. Believe me I did, but they said they didn't know, and then they hit me, on the neck, like that." He made a chopping motion.

"Don't worry, it's over now, Jeno. They won't do it again." There was a little lush island in the lake. Sheep were grazing, and beyond the sheep was a clump of trees that had openings into mysterious darkness. Jeno was nervous again getting out of the boat. Hugo had a basket and spread cakes and sandwiches on a faded blue sheet. Jeno insisted on eating a sandwich from his own canvas bag, in which he still kept his prized possessions: letters, his breviary, a transistor radio on which he constantly listened to the chatter of disc jockeys.

"At least take coffee."

"No, Hugo, that's not allowed — you know that." They lay in the sun, side by side. Hugo wanted, for ever and ever, to soak up the presence of Jeno, once his best friend, in a world where fate had allowed him so few friends. Jeno fell asleep, whimpering at times, back in the camp; all he had to do to return there was fall asleep. It wasn't me; Fust would have sent him away in any case, the other voice in Hugo's head said. But that voice carried no conviction.

"The trouble is, Jeno," he said as the boat took them back to shore, "I have this huge decision to make, and the only one I can talk to about it is you."

"I understand, Hugo."

"Do you really think there's a God, Jeno?"

"Don't talk so loud, Hugo. They might be listening."

"Are you — are you happy, Jeno?"

"It was you got me out, Hugo. You're my best friend."

The boat glided effortlessly over the water. The earth was never more beautiful than on that lake that day, Hugo thought. Nor ever more sad. He and the real Jeno had said their good-bye years ago. He would have to decide alone who he would be for the rest of his life.

He was sitting in his favorite chair and saying the divine office late into the night — still taking selective stabs at being the best priest walking the earth, in private as well as in public. More than that, the rhythmic poetry of the Jewish songs and the belief of the people who wrote them had become part of him with time and repetition, songs passed on not only in print but by osmosis from one century of believers to the next. The psalms appealed most strongly when the world was bleak, as it was now, offering a possible alternative with God as shepherd leading a motley flock to where there were green pastures. He was tired after the day on the lake with Jeno.

A slow car entered his yard pouring light through his window. He knew who it was. He went to meet her at the door. "You're full of surprises."

"I know you said not to come back."

"What's the matter, Eva? I have cold coffee."

"You're in danger, Hugo."

"You must be mistaken."

"Do you know a man named Herzeg?"

"Imre?"

"Then you know I'm not inventing it."

She looked anxiously through the window to where her car was parked. She seemed vulnerable in a way he had never seen her before. Now that he was over the shock of what the twenty-five years had done to them both, she looked more beautiful than last time. She had never married. Like himself. She deserved a shot at marriage. They could still make a run for it as they had once dreamed of doing.

"Were you followed? You have put yourself in danger by coming here."

"I'll take that cold coffee." He took her arm and guided her into the study. "Straight," she said. He went and got it. She sat on the arm of his big chair.

"What else do you know about me?"

"All I know is that there was more than you told me, but I don't know exactly what. And right now it doesn't matter." She held out the big brown mug for more coffee and he poured it. She looked him in the eye, and he looked back at her. It did not matter, he thought, whether the word for it was love or something else. It was unique. And would last both their lifetimes. Now he knew that her previous visit had had a purpose beyond explaining her strange youthful decision. They had never, as the saying was, gone to bed together, yet when two people had met as intimately as they had, this affected their lives ever after, put an imprint on them, even if they never were to meet again.

"There's nothing I can do, Eva."

"You could leave the country."

His only hope now, he was thinking with mild amusement, sitting there with his life in jeopardy and the one love of his life within arm's length yet out of his reach, was that there might be a God. There and then Hugo presumed it would not be an angry God standing by the red-hot gates to lock him up and stoke him later. Rather it would be a well-rounded God who could take a joke and enjoy the farce of him limping through life with his sack of uncertainties on his back, a God with a touch of appreciation for an old fart of a fake bishop who yet sat up late at night reading psalms even when no one save God was looking. A mellow God apologizing for not having cleared up Hugo's dilemma. And in a moment of grand forgiveness wiping away the blood of Sandor and the betrayal of Jeno. One could only hope.

"It's too late for leaving the country. I have a rendezvous with Imre tomorrow."

"You could leave. I can help you."

"Too dangerous. Get out of here." A life really criss-crosses only a few others out of the millions on earth. It was foolish to look for a pattern, yet a few lives like Eva's converged with his again and again; it was impossible to say when anything was over or when a good-bye was the last.

"Listen to me, Hugo." She stood to go as she put down her coffee mug with purpose. "It will be my gift. I am in a position to do it, and it will make up for, you know, the past. You know what I mean?" She held out her hand. He took it, and they held hands for a whole minute. They were past fifty and tired. Love was wasted on the young. It was past fifty that the touch of a hand was needed. The lucky ones were those still holding hands after surviving the love they risked in their youth.

In a few deft words she told him what he needed to do, then walked out with head straight without looking back. The lights of her car waved good-bye to him back inside in his study.

Dawn was still an hour away as Hugo drove out of the yard of the bishop's house on Thursday morning. Dunauvaros was sleeping except for an occasional car crawling around corners and a milkman with wire baskets and noisy glass bottles. Hugo had left a note for the housekeeper: "Gone to the lake — all appointments canceled."

He doubled back briefly to satisfy himself that no car was following. A policeman stepped out from a corner, and Hugo slammed on the brakes, but the cop crossed the street in defiance of the red light.

Several miles out of town he stopped on a quiet stretch of road. He waited to ensure that no one was out or about in the still world.

He extracted a bundle from the trunk of the car, the dungarees and denim jacket of a factory worker and the boots and cloth cap of a peasant. He pulled off the roman collar. He stuffed the clerical shoes and clothes in a cloth bag. He climbed down an embankment beside the little bridge and threw the bag in the water, watched it sink.

It was a routine he had prepared twenty years ago and rehearsed in his mind ever since. He made mud with a handkerchief and smeared it on the shiny, clean car. He looked around, on constant alert. He had not shaved before leaving. In his wallet he had an identity card to match his new appearance — once given to him by Fust in case of necessity. Life was ironic. He drove on.

By daylight he was on the outskirts of Komarom and heading west. Between Komarom and Gyor the gas needle was dipping dangerously low. He eased the car into a quiet gas station.

"A fine car you have there, friend." The attendant was an old man with a lazy eye.

"Yeah, but she's a devil on gas."

"I'd be prepared to buy if you were prepared to sell."

"Not today." The man continued to eye the car. He would remember it if there were questions later.

"Where do you come from, friend?"

"Heygeshalom. I'm on my way home." Hugo pushed the money into the man's hand.

"Lived there for twenty years. She needs a wash." He hated to see Hugo's car get away. "Yeah, twenty years. If you were from Heygeshalom, friend, I'd know you."

At eight the music on the radio was interrupted for the morning news. There were reports about the economy, a new factory opening, a bank robbery in Pozsony. And then the news that Eva was dead. Her car had met with an accident, the announcer said.

Then the music was back on the radio, so that Hugo wondered if he had heard correctly or only imagined the news. He had slowed the car spontaneously. A van hooted behind him before moving with a fuss past him. Still he slowed, his life grinding to a halt. If he heard what he thought he heard, then her death was no accident.

He pulled over on the grassy shoulder. He knew he looked conspicuous as the morning traffic thickened. Let them catch him. He turned off the sassy, mocking music. He lowered his head to rest on the steering wheel. Cry, damn you. It was his fault, nothing could be more obvious. It was for him she did it. Went, in effect, to her death.

Even as she told him of his danger she was glancing out the window at her own danger. How could he have let her take such a risk? Yet he could not cry, holding the wheel with his knuckles white, his eyes closed and searching inside himself for the faintest trace of sentiment or feeling, for any trace of a heart, but finding nothing.

If they caught him he would ask to be shot at the old monastery. In the early morning. He would demand it. At once, on the heels of Eva. He banged his head on the steering wheel, which gave him comfort. He began to hope. If they shot him by that old wall at dawn, it would make the world perfect again, redress every wrong he had done to it. The world would then be in at least as good a shape as before he arrived to screw it up. And he would catch up with Eva before she had gone half a mile toward heaven or wherever the road led.

And still he could not cry. At last he opened his eyes. It was full bright morning. Trucks were taking men to work. A man was driving cows from a field. Hugo promised himself he would grieve later if he ever found a place where he could be human again. There was some ineffable kind of victory here — he could not let it be a defeat or meaningless; it was something elevated above the sordid life he had always known. It was a life given for a friend — so biblical and therefore ironic when it happened to him of all people. Eva lived on somewhere; that much had to be true. It might well be, as Fust insisted, that there was no afterlife, but either way his mother and Eva, at least, lived on, exceptions. Everyone was allowed a few exceptions.

He passed a road sign that said "Gyor." He pulled over and chewed on a sandwich from a brown bag. It tasted like sand, but he needed to survive. When he wrote the definitive history of the world, that would be the climactic chapter: how they first stole the happiness Eva had planned to live with her son and Hugo in a little house wrapped around with flowers; and then killed her with the touch of his hand almost warm on hers.

If what he had heard was true, tomorrow would be the funeral. He would not be there to afford her the traditional Catholic stab at heaven, even assuming she desired it. But he was sure there was a side door off to the left of St. Peter's pearly gate where a limping angel would beckon her and shake her hand again and give her a smack on the cheek and a pat on the backside and let her through when God's back was turned.

When he had finished eating he found a phone and made a phone call.

An hour later, the sign said "Customs," and he slowed to a crawl. The official, who had a bulldog face, stooped down to look in the window with the usual scrutiny, his trained eye taking in everything.

"What is your destination?"

"Pozsony," Hugo said.

"Let me see your license."

"I'm afraid I forgot it. But I can show you my identity card."

"You need a license. Please step out." Hugo felt stiff from the long drive. He stretched, trying to be casual. He was puzzled: this was not according to plan. "That's a mighty fine car," the bulldog said. "Open the trunk."

Hugo did as he was told.

"I'll deal with it," another official said behind them. "It's taken care of," the bulldog said.

"I said I'd deal with it." The newcomer was testy and the bulldog obviously a subordinate who now slunk away. The new official went through the motions of searching the trunk.

"You'll have no trouble," he said. "Once you get over the bridge, you are free."

"I'm very grateful," Hugo said, speaking low and terse like the official. "My God, you're Arthur!" he said once he got a look at him.

The official, filling out forms on the bonnet of the car, ignored his surprise. "Here, sign this."

Hugo signed the paper. He was mesmerized. Her son. She had just died and he was on duty. The world was small and also upside down. Arthur was holding the door for him, and, puzzled, he eased himself back behind the wheel.

"Well, I think that's everything," Arthur said officiously, bending closer.

"Didn't you hear?"

"I heard," Arthur said.

"Good God. It's true, then."

"Control yourself." He was curt again. "Your life may depend on it."

For a brief moment they removed their invisible public masks and looked directly at each other.

"Did you know...?"

"Yeah, you were going to teach me soccer. She told me." He put the mask on again without another word and waved Hugo's car forward. The bridge was directly ahead. Only yards away. Once you get over the bridge you are free, Arthur had said. But there were soldiers everywhere. It was disheartening. If the country was the Paradise the Party promised, were these soldiers keeping people in or out of Paradise? He put the question on hold. He drove very slowly. The smallest wrong move could spell trouble or death. He drove past the first soldiers, then other soldiers, then onto the bridge. No soldier paid any special attention. They might be waiting to kill him as he reached the other side, setting up an international incident. He drove a little faster, as the heavy boards of the bridge rattled. The more he drove the longer the bridge stretched ahead. But a moment finally came when he was at the other side, and not dead. Freedom. He slowed down. He could drive leisurely through freedom.

Many hours and miles later, another signpost said "Vienna." In the city, he drove aimlessly with the traffic until he came to a shopping center. He parked the car, then locked it carefully. Still in his old working clothes, he went from window to window until he saw what he wanted. He came out wearing an elegant gray suit and a blue tie.

He drove again until he found a hotel. He locked himself in his room. He wedged a chair under the door handle as an added precaution. He went to the window, looked out at the lights of the city. Above the tall shoulders of skyscrapers shone a full moon. He watched it until it grew larger and more alive — he had told her he would think of her whenever he saw it.

He threw himself on the bed and finally broke down into uncontrollable sobbing — the grief of his entire lifetime spilling out. At the right moment to cry was so sweet, the pain a pleasure.

He fell asleep from exhaustion. When he awoke the room was full of sunshine. He looked out the window and the moon was gone. Good-bye, Eva.

Later, he drove to the airport. He found a parking space under a tree. He locked the car carefully. As he walked to the terminal he observed the people going about their business. One was a woman begging near the big glass door. He handed her the key. He pointed to his car in the far distance. "It's yours," he told her, "I don't need it anymore."

"I don't need it either," she said, and threw the key away. Whoever eventually fixed the world would, first of all, have to restore trust.

Hugo bought a one-way ticket to Rome. Looking down over the city, he could see only clouds. It's symbolic, he thought. Whatever it means. He felt light and free.

Chapter Twenty

Bishop Hugo Ovath, dressed in his new gray suit and blue tie, held out a handful of money, and the Roman taxi driver took what seemed an inordinate amount of it and then drove away. He'll get killed, Hugo thought. Every day that a driver survived in Rome was another miracle and proof positive that the Catholic Church was the one and only, the American Conlon had joked. Hugo was afloat on a sea of euphoria.

He made a phone call. Then he climbed the steps to a fountain in front of St. Peter's Basilica. The sun had moved around and cast the facade in shadows. No matter what people said about the magnificence of St. Peter's, the experience itself topped every expectation. Hugo sat on a stone step in the heat of the day. He scanned the crowds who hauled their backpacks from wonder to wonder on this pilgrim trail.

"Ladislaus!"

The familiar figure came forward, slower now, but with the welcoming arm outstretched and in the other hand the pipe that Hugo felt he seldom filled any more but carried around as a wand to wave at life.

"In the name of God, Hugo, what is going on?" This time he spread his arms in Roman fashion and greeted Hugo with a hug. "Your phone call scared the wits out of me."

"I hate that old hugging, Ladislaus. What's wrong with shaking hands?"

"Are you being followed?" Ladislaus was agitated. He looked suspiciously at passing pilgrims. He was wearing the quaint, wide-brimmed, round-topped hat that Italian clerics traditionally wore.

"May I say just one thing, Ladislaus? I know I'm new in Rome,

– 156 –

but that is a really ugly hat, and I don't think you should be obliged to wear it."

"How did you get out?" Ladislaus started walking and Hugo followed.

"I drove. If you don't believe me, you'll find my grand car at the Vienna airport. I tried to give it away, but no one would take it."

"Slow down, Hugo," Ladislaus said, although he was striding three steps ahead of Hugo. "I don't understand this at all."

"It's a long story...."

Before the main altar of St. Peter's Basilica the old, frail pope sat on his throne dwarfed by Bernini's famous canopy and all the huge statues of his papal predecessors wearing triple tiaras and threatening humanity with damnation. Dignitaries from around the world filled the choir stalls. A television camera blinked incongruously on a tall scaffolding by a window. Music swelled as the cardinals-to-be shuffled down the broad center aisle, out of step with each other and the music. Two were whispering. Another was looking up at the television camera. They were wayward and perverse and impossible to organize, but it was after all their day — the consistory.

"I'm happy to meet you," an American had said to Hugo as they dressed in their finery in an adjacent sacristy, a brilliant room with fine frescoes of its own, perhaps created by Michelangelo or his helpers doing practice runs for the nearby Sistine Chapel. "You have made great strides with the Communists," the friendly American continued.

"Thank you." Hugo was grateful for the long nights he had spent studying English.

"And I have read your books. You bring a fresh new perspective to the thorny issues of church-state relations." Hugo thanked him profusely. He wanted to ask many questions about Philadelphia and Cleveland and Baltimore, but a hush was settling and a sallow master of ceremonies was clapping his soft hands for attention. "Your Communists are not as ruthless as our dictators," a black cardinal from Africa had said to Hugo the day before. He had not known what to say. He had a thousand opinions but few that he was confident enough to air in this new arena. He had no right to be here.

"Veni, Creator Spiritus" was intoned by the Sistine Choir. It was the music to which they shuffled, music dusted off from the attic of history and paraded on every big church occasion. Inspiring words climbed on soaring notes until it began to seem possible that the Creator Spirit might indeed come down and do damage control on earth and especially clear away the anarchical clutter of Hugo's mind. If God were to wipe the slate clean, Hugo thought, he himself might be prepared to go on his knees in earnest and begin all over again. If there were a God, that is — he'd worry about that later.

Long prayers were said and a litany was chanted and incense burned and bells rung. In the middle of it all Hugo's mind wandered. No doubt, so does the pope's mind wander, he consoled himself; that's how human we all are. If there is something worthwhile happening, it is happening in spite of us humans.

Eventually they were walking forward. Then the hand of the pope was on his hand. He, once a rebellious peasant from the mountains. The pope's cheek touched his cheek in the awkward old Roman salutation; he wished they would settle for a handshake. He looked into the old man's sad eyes. On that throne he must feel the weight of the big bad world — no one could blame him if he let his mind wander at times. Although it was also said that the office of pope lifted up every man who sat on it. Maybe gave him the weird wisdom to call Hugo here — the Creator Spirit laughing up his invisible sleeve.

Rome still loved a circus. When the new cardinals emerged in their spiffy regalia, foreign journalists surrounded Hugo, the enigma, the man with a limp who broke an old impasse with the Communists, a man who spoke for the freedom fighters back in '57 and even went to jail. And because they could not explain him, they tried the harder.

"Your Eminence, given the philosophical, theological, and ideological presuppositions on which each is based, would it not be fair to hypothesize that the Communist-Christian dichotomy is an irreconcilable one?"

At the Catholic University of Chicago, a thousand students and their teachers had turned out to hear Hugo deliver a lecture on East-West relations.

"Your Eminence, are Communists not secretly religious, making a religion out of nonreligion?"

"Eminence, will Christianity survive under Communism?"

"Is it true that you were once a Communist?"

They were interested in random knowledge. Children of prosperity, they knew so little of the bleak, wintry side of life, especially as it was lived beyond their own shores. They were unfairly protected to chew their gum and drive their Mustangs, growing soft as a race. So sure of themselves, theirs was a false security. If they did not scratch their own surfaces for deeper meaning, they would some day wake up to find themselves poor and maybe concentration camps across their land. Theirs was fertile ground for the devious incursions of some future Fust with a gimmick whose time would have come.

"Your Eminence, have the reforms of the Second Vatican Council reached your neck of the woods yet?"

"What is the purpose of your trip, Eminence?"

"You could call it a fact-finding trip. As director of the Secretariat for Non-Christians, I am naturally eager to learn more about the diversity of the West."

He had thrown himself into the life and work of the Roman curia. In his Vatican apartment, which oozed the history of centuries of Catholicism, stories of intrigue and miracles of grace, his light was the last one to go out at night. He devoured the history and culture of his new world. He polished the languages and practiced them on every foreigner who would talk to him. He had also, he realized one day, grown light-hearted, less gloomy and intense.

It's having Fust off my back, he would conclude. But Fust wasn't the worst of them, he would add. Fust was the best of them. That was the problem — the rest of them.

In the first weeks and months he had waited for an outcry from home. They would pick the right moment to expose him and in a double whammy disgrace the church. He scanned the papers, listened to the radio, but there was a stunning silence. Then it dawned on him that the Party, meanwhile, might be waiting in its own trepidation for Hugo to spill the beans. It was hard to say who was cat and who was mouse.

He was the logical choice to head the Secretariat for Non-Christians. It made sense to make a whirlwind tour of South and then North America.

And on to Washington, where the local cardinal gave him a hero's welcome and arranged for his appearance on the *Jimmy Hudson Show*.

"Jimmy can be very aggressive, but you can handle it," the cardinal said. "Besides, Senator Knoll will be on the panel. He's a Catholic and a good friend of mine; he won't let Jimmy hassle you."

"Jimmy may try to hassle you," the senator said at the studio, "but the trick is to interrupt him if you don't like where he's going."

"I don't understand what you mean, hassle."

"You'll know it when you see it," said Sandy Morris, a large woman, a feminist who was said to have strong views about the role of women in the church. The other member of the panel was a young priest with a black turtleneck sweater and an aggressive mustache. They all looked like cheap porcelain in their makeup.

"Cardinal Ovath," Jimmy Hudson began when they were on the air. "In 1957, in a speech to the freedom-fighters of Dunauvaros, you said, and I quote, 'When freedom is achieved, we can all live together, Communist and Christian, in harmony and prosperity.' Did Your Eminence really believe that?"

"Yes, I believed it." Hugo did not remember having said it in the first place.

Then Jimmy sprang his surprise: an old grainy film showing Hugo making one of his speeches during the 1957 uprising. It was stunning to realize that all this time his role was preserved; it caused him to wonder what else people knew. "You are also alleged to have said you would lead the people in their fight until all their demands had been met. Is that correct?"

"You have a better memory than I."

"Then what are you doing here?" This was the abrasive edge on which Jimmy's reputation rested. The senator moved in to protect Hugo. "I submit that the cardinal is still leading the people's fight," he pontificated until Jimmy in desperation kicked the young priest for a contribution.

"Some say that all you have over there, Cardinal, is an outmoded church that, well, never caught up with the twentieth century."

Hugo briefly contemplated giving Jimmy a show that would be talked about as long as people talked about television: all he had to do was beat the crap out of this saucy young priest and then pull out the holy oils and anoint him before he died a holy death in front of the cameras.

"We haven't heard from you, Sandy." Jimmy didn't realize that Hugo was contemplating a television "event" for posterity.

"He's so cute," Sandy said. "I can't bring myself to say all the horrible things I had planned to say. But I do think he should do something about the celibacy thing. It's such a waste." She was smoking a long black cigarillo. She went on to say a few more horrible things anyway, including the fact that, after hundreds of male popes, it was time for at least one female pope. Hugo was fascinated by the extreme length of her fingernails. He wondered why the people who were invited on shows like Jimmy Hudson's were so seldom typical people, but then he realized he was scarcely the right one to complain. The producer was making signals to Jimmy from behind a curtain.

"Cardinal Ovath, it's no secret that your name has been mentioned as a candidate for the papacy. Would you care to comment on that?" The senator smiled benignly. So did Sandy. America was such a generous country. People liked other people and wished them well for the most part and were open to almost anything. They wouldn't flinch at a Communist pope — so long as it was a Communist they liked.

"That's a silly question, Mr. Hudson." Hugo had decided to put Jimmy in his box. "And right now I can't think of a silly answer."

"We say to God, 'Show me and I will enter.' But God says, 'No, enter and I will show you.'"

Someone called McHale had written that, the retreat master said. The retreat master was a straight, rigid man with a high forehead and crinkly hair. He was always quoting someone, Thomas Aquinas or Kierkegaard or Jesus or unknown people like McHale. Then he would pause and stare at his audience. He loved to pause.

Hugo had decided to make a retreat in America before returning to Rome. Already he had some regrets. The brooding retreat master kept lobbing low-intensity thunderbolts at his audience. Giving God bright new ideas that Hugo thought might not have crossed God's mind before. Enter and I will show you. Putting the burden on humans, the small fry, to make the first move. The most Hugo had ever conceded was he might believe if God were to pull a wild stunt such as walking on water, and it would have to be deep water at that.

He was making the retreat to help his image. There must be, he now realized, an easier way.

The retreat house in the hills outside New York was an old mansion once owned by a tycoon who built railways. A new wing was added in gray brick, as well as a new round chapel with chunky colored glass windows blood red for the crucifixion and light blue for God's mother, or perhaps it was for the sky over one's native mountains. One could take symbols down any old road.

It was a no-nonsense retreat. He was locked in for six days with twenty-eight others: priests; eight Sisters, including one called Francine who had a gold tooth and who always managed to sit beside Hugo at table asking questions, needing the attention more than the answers; and a lone lay deacon who was an undertaker in real life.

Most of them wanted to be, for the six days at least, one big happy family. They talked continually about "sharing," while Hugo, restless after two high-powered weeks in the public eye of one city after another, was afraid of them opening their private hearts to him. And even more afraid of opening his to them. Or opening his to himself. He walked alone by the river while the others walked in twos and threes. The leaves had turned beautiful colors in the fall of the year. This made him melancholy. Everything and everyone turned most beautiful and lovable just in time for departure and death.

"At any moment people must decide, for better or worse, what will be the monument of their existence," the priest quoted Victor Frankl. Afterward, in the balmy evening, a sliver of moon lay on its back over the river. It shone for everyone; distance did not matter — if there was someone you loved you could send a message and they would read it tomorrow pale in a different sky.

The sound of a guitar came from the gray wing of the house, strummed, Hugo knew, by a priest in his forties who had a golden voice but did not seek to be noticed or praised. "And they'll know we are Christians by our love, by our love," he sang, and the sound floated down to the river and up to the moon.

"Two men sit facing each other and both of them are me. Quietly, meticulously, systematically, they are blowing out each other's brains," the retreat master quoted R. D. Laing. Now Hugo was certain the priest was looking at him: two men and no man, his brains meticulously blown out years ago — whether in seminary or summer camp he wasn't sure.

"The desire that is satisfied is not a great desire," he quoted Yeats on Wednesday night. And he went on with his coaxing, glowing picture of peace down here and glory in heaven. Hugo had to admit that he was more than the sum of his quotations. He was a good witness. He was not faking. He would be genuinely devastated to die and see a sign at the top of heaven's high ladder, "Out of Business."

They asked Hugo to be the main celebrant for Mass on Thursday evening. The priest played his guitar, and his voice was powerful and free and still flying to the moon. Hugo preached a short, uninspired homily. They dragged out the kiss-of-peace ceremony at the end. Sister Francine said it was a lovely talk he gave, so he went for a walk with her. He thought of telling her they were only words and he was not sure of their meaning. But he had once told Fust that if he could not make the world any better he ought not to make it worse. He listened to the tinkle of Francine's voice and learned that she was once engaged to a quiet, sympathetic man but broke it off to become a nun and was now a teacher of mathematics.

There were only two days left for confession, the retreat master said. On Friday evening, when grace seemed to be running through the house like a mad mountain torrent, Hugo thought he might try him. It was safe. His lips were sealed by the sacrament. Hugo might pick up some of the contentment he saw in the faces of the others. There was no limit to God's forgiveness — that was the guarantee. If God turned out to be only a mirage, then nothing was lost. Except sweat, Hugo's, as he walked by the river and fought with himself. He was convinced that if he did it, he could then live with himself only if he followed the rules. Not just the external ones — he had promised that and kept the promise as well as any priest alive, he thought without pride — but the internal ones. He would have to mean it. If he couldn't mean it, he would have to will to mean it. It was daunting.

Down and back he walked, looking up at the lighted window where the retreat master was waiting. It was a matter of turning his face in that direction, putting one foot in front of the other.

Yet he could not do it. He turned and went the other way. He was not able to mean it enough. A train roared past beyond the river, carrying capitalists. They were no longer his enemies. They and he were all people.

"You must come to the party, Eminence," Francine said.

It was Saturday evening, and they would all be parting in the morning. The retreat master became human again after his week on the job, wearing a blue sweater, smoking a cigar, a can of beer in his hand, the penetrating stare taking a rest.

The priest with the guitar played, and they all sang together. Hugo noticed that the singing priest was drinking a large quantity of beer. Two of the sisters danced, but none of the men volunteered to dance with them.

"I hate to go back into the world," a bald man said.

"What do you do?"

"I'm in charge of the seminary."

"Did you know that I too used to be in charge of a seminary?"

"Are you kidding? We know everything about you."

The priest with the guitar got drunk and began shouting. The great voice was housed in an all-too-human body. But the others were kind to him. Patient. Love was more than a word; it was a reality, a something that made the pain bearable for the world going round.

Chapter Twenty-One

In the middle of an otherwise quiet night Hugo was awakened by a knock on his door. "Who is it?" he grumbled in the darkness.

The door opened until Cardinal Pogioli was a silhouette against the light of the corridor. The silhouette was wearing pajamas.

"The Holy Father is dead," Pogioli said. There was a silence. It was the sort of news that needed time to sink in. Then Hugo turned on the bedside lamp and swung his feet to the floor.

"Like a thief in the night, Pogioli."

"The poor old bastard went quickly after all," Pogioli said. "Have you anything to drink?"

"I know where there's coffee."

"It will be another bureaucrat; you'll see," Pogioli said.

"No, they'll be looking for a shepherd type who believes in God and the power of love and all that." Hugo pulled on a brown robe. He looked at himself in a mirror on the wall beside his bed. He ran fingers through his hair, then patted it down. "Has everyone been told?" He knew well how news like this seeped through the Vatican corridors, even in the middle of the night, and then leaped out over the media to the shocked world.

The body lay in state in St. Peter's, dressed in red chasuble, red slippers, white gloves, white miter trimmed with gold, in front of the high altar and Bernini's canopy, the very place where he sat when he welcomed Hugo as a cardinal and a prince of the church. Four Swiss Guards kept watch, dressed in the gaudy uniforms designed for them long ago by Michelangelo.

"I hate conclaves," an old cardinal who had been at the last one said. The old man, Hugo, and two other members of the curia were out walking after dinner. His problem with conclaves, the old man said, was being away from his bed, which matched the contours of his body.

Hugo reminded him that the electing cardinals were locked up in the Sistine Chapel precisely to keep them from being comfortable. Until such measures were taken, there had often been political shenanigans at conclaves. The old cardinal passed gas.

"Carfino is getting all the attention," an archbishop said. Carfino was a front-runner, a wily diplomat who had spent most of his life in the curia, abrasive and self-important. Hugo did not like him.

"He's the curia's man; he'll be suspect," another said. There was a traditional divide between the curia in Rome, the bureaucrats who ruled the church, and the workers in the field, which was a big field, the whole world, who had their own limited autonomy but usually grumbled quietly against directives coming from Rome. It was not as simple as that, of course. People found many ways to divide themselves at a time like this. They were unpredictable men in their own right, endowed with some sort of independence that helped them rise to their present eminence, but even this was compounded by the belief that God too took a hand in the decision. And indeed history offered many examples that were hard to explain without outside intervention.

Hugo sat on a wall by Rome's renowned Trevi Fountain, reading a book. He was dressed in his gray suit. Tourists came by, took pictures, threw coins in the water, giggled, and made wishes with their eyes closed, often kissed those they loved in this magnificent monument to love. In the distance a sharp eye would have picked out Fust, an umbrella in one hand, a briefcase in the other, wearing a casual jacket and a sporty brown hat.

At sight of Hugo, Fust stopped. They looked at each other. He looks older, Hugo thought. But, no doubt, so do I. Hugo remained seated. Fust came forward again, stopped again, two or three more times, like an animal approaching its prey, until he was in front of Hugo, still sitting, looking up at the new arrival.

"Your Eminence?"

"Why, Zoltan? Why couldn't you leave it alone?"

"I'm sorry to bother you, Hugo. It's been — oh, it's been so long."

"Who's with you?" A few days earlier, he had received a cable with the terse message: "Arriving Rome Airport Tuesday at two — Uncle Georg."

"May I sit down?" He sat at a little distance, the case and umbrella perched on his lap. At times tourists walked between them,
interrupting them. "Imre is with me."

"Why wouldn't you let Ladislaus come for the funeral?" Hugo had
talked to him on the phone. Ladislaus said he had even tried to phone
Hugo's friend, Madach, but was told there was no such person.

"Not my decision, Hugo."

"Are we being watched? I mean, right now?"

"I don't know," Fust said. "But if you want my opinion, there are
anywhere from two to four sets of eyes devoted fully to us, and at
least one gun is pointed in our general direction, and I'm honestly not
sure if it's concentrated on you or me."

An American tourist apologized and asked Hugo to take a photo of
himself and his wife. Hugo coaxed them to tilt their faces to catch the
sun. They beamed their gratitude. Hugo sat closer to Fust on the wall.

"What do you want, Zoltan?"

"There's so much unfinished business. I'd have left you in peace,
but not Imre."

"Imre runs it, huh?"

"Imre's the man. He still has those thin wrists. He's minister of the
interior now — you must have heard that." The once-indomitable Fust
sighed his resignation. "What can I do, Hugo? I have no other life."

"You used to have backbone, Zoltan. Not to mention imagination. . . ."

"We'd better go." He stood up, and Hugo did likewise and followed
Fust, who still walked with all the public swagger of the old days —
he must, Hugo thought, be knocking on seventy.

". . . Imagination and some sort of integrity," Hugo went on. "Not
the usual kind, Zoltan, you had an integrity all your own."

Zoltan and Imre were staying in a first-class hotel.

"So good to see you," Imre said when he saw Hugo, being polite,
even friendly.

"Doesn't His Eminence look well?" Fust commented. Whatever
was to happen, Fust was eager to make it work smoothly.

"Zoltan loves saying that — Your Eminence. Your departure was
very sudden — Your Eminence." There was an imperceptible change
in Imre's tone.

"I made a deal with Zoltan before you were born, and I kept it until you interfered. It cost me a lot, nearly everything that most people cherish in life, but I did it. And then you came along. . . ."

"Please. No use getting upset." There was a living room that seemed to lead to two bedrooms. Hugo recalled Imre's plants and how he talked to them on that bitter day. There were no plants in this room except a box on the window ledge, as there seemed to be on every ledge in Rome. "Do sit down. What would you like to drink?"

"Get on with it." Hugo made no effort to be friendly. The imperturbable Imre poured a drink for Fust, then one for himself. He stood with his back to the window.

"I'm sorry if Your Eminence does not like me, but I can't help the way I am. And I didn't make the world the way it is, and as we all know it's sometimes a bitch. . . ."

"It was less of a bitch before you came along."

"We understand that you are — how do they pronounce it? — papabile."

"What do you want?"

"Well, naturally, if you were pope, we would like — I hope it doesn't sound selfish, but we would like you to be our pope."

"I'm not going to be pope."

"Modesty befitting a pope!"

"Trust me."

"You can at least influence the outcome."

"Yes, we have heard great things, Hugo." Fust too wanted to resurrect the hope of the halcyon days.

"Sorry, Zoltan. Even if I could I wouldn't help you."

"Are you saying — have you gone over to them, Hugo? Are you saying you believe?" He was leaning forward in the chair, the classic Fust posture. He had downed the glass of brandy and poured another.

"That's the mistake we made, Zoltan. We believed in belief. Our heads were full of belief and ideology. If it wasn't the church, it had to be the Party. But as the years go on, our allegiance goes not to the beliefs but to the people who embody them. Me — I got trapped with the people in the church. They rubbed off on me. They're a mixture of good and bad like everyone else, but now I'm one of them."

"And their God?" Imre pretended to sip his drink.

"I don't know about God. It would be really easy if I knew about God."

"It's so complicated, Hugo." Imre moved closer. "Surely we can somehow be friends. To show my good will, I'll have your Ladislaus cleared this very day. He could be here in a couple of days."

"And in return?"

"In return — nothing. It's our gift."

"Please, Hugo," Fust too was eager. "We've waited so long for a payday."

"Please, Zoltan, don't drool," Imre said. "Ladislaus will be at the airport tomorrow at four," he said to Hugo. "I promise it."

Ladislaus came down the airport ramp, right hand out. He put the pipe in his pocket in order to embrace Hugo, who took the canvas bag hanging from his shoulder.

"It could be a long conclave, Ladislaus. You'll need more clothes than you could possibly put in this."

"All I need is underwear and toothpaste. I have enough of both for a month." They rode back to Rome on a crowded bus, past ancient landmarks.

"What about Pogioli?"

"No chance."

"Nadalet, then?"

"For God's sake, Ladislaus, light that pipe and relax." He lit the pipe and smoke swirled. He fixed Hugo with a sharp eye: "I heard some of the foreigners were going to vote for you."

"They'll be wasting their votes." The smoke on the bus grew thicker. Other passengers moved away, too polite to tell a prince of the church to stick his pipe somewhere else.

Not for nothing was the history of the papacy so colorful and laced with intrigue and dark rumors as well as bright intervals — popes made a hell of an imprint on the world.

Whether the imprint stretched beyond space and time to heaven or eternity was another matter. Hugo, mountain peasant, still stooped under the rubble of skepticism, had haunted old Rome in search of clues. From catacombs to basilicas to an odd pagan temple or section of cobbled street away from the tourist trail where a little-known cleric once had an insight or a martyr died, he limped in search of significance.

He sensed a pervasive schizophrenia. They were Christians, they said, but Hugo noticed that Rome was less a Christian town than a papal town. While most religions focused overwhelmingly on their particular deity, or the founder or prophet who brought them into existence, when Catholicism was mentioned the first concept to pop into most minds, Catholic or non-Catholic, was its temporal leader, the reigning pope.

Great though some of those popes may have been, Hugo had a hunch that the serious searcher ought to be wandering instead by the Sea of Galilee and on the little roads Jesus walked. As many indeed did. But for most pilgrims, a two-thousand-year succession of popes had eclipsed the founder.

This message was writ large on Rome's churches and monuments. These were built either by this pope or that or in honor of him. The message was carved near doors everywhere, including the pagan Pantheon. Even the beautiful Trevi Fountain, a stone poem to more human love — Hugo was sad to see, across the facade, two popes, one of the Clements and one of the Benedicts, boast to posterity how one of them began and the other finished the monument.

Perhaps it wasn't the popes' fault. There were always fawning underlings to organize homage to the powerful. Popes, being human, perhaps did not wish to reprimand such ardent followers, and in any case it was always pleasant to see one's name in stone for the ages.

The dilemma was most obvious in the magnificent St. Peter's, where St. Peter's Chair, a bronze creation by the renowned artist Bernini, reigned as the prestigious focal point behind the main altar. In humbler churches around the world, the deity, usually hanging from a cross, held this place of honor.

It seemed paradoxically logical to Hugo, as it allegedly had seemed to Jesus, that if popes genuinely wanted to inherit the earth, they should be more meek and humble.

The art in St. Peter's was likewise legendary. But while many of the subjects were saints, Hugo noticed the majority were popes. And not the humble popes one might expect followers of the humble Jesus to be. Most were power popes, wearing triple tiaras and hands outstretched in imperious command. Fust would make a better pope than himself, Hugo thought. At least the Fust of old would. The Fust of old would have worn that heavy tiara lightly, with a swagger.

Unless there was, in truth, a divine dimension, a mystical shore, a rock of Peter beyond the beyond. On which the all-too-earthly Fust would soon be shipwrecked.

Only a day had elapsed when Hugo had been summoned again to Imre's towering hotel and told he would, after all, have to spill the beans of his duplicity to the wide world. Just when he had grown used to freedom, he felt the same old noose tightening around his neck.

"Things have changed." Imre was sitting in a high chair in the middle of the room, looking out the window, his back to Hugo. Fust was sulking at the side and drinking vodka.

"And you really think, Imre, that if I get up there and tell everyone how we fooled the church — you are so naive, my friend. This would hardly cause a blip in the history of the church. They glide over scandals like a swan over water."

"Hugo is right." Fust came to life. "Compared to the long-term advantages of working together . . ."

"Oh, shut up, Zoltan."

Hugo looked over at Fust with a sort of pity. Giving up on him. On Uncle Georg who once had panache in every pocket. The resourceful diabolical Commie with an ace up every sleeve, now fallen so far. Exasperated, Hugo made no effort to hide the pity, knowing full well that pity would finish Fust for good.

"And if I refuse?" he said to Imre.

"We'll hold the press conference and expose you anyway."

"Where are those orders coming from?"

"That scarcely matters."

"It matters a lot, Imre, my boy."

History, most of the time, turns on small events, often unknown to the world ever after. The time and the person and a few circumstances come together at a propitious crossroads. And, sometimes, a gun appears. From under his coat Fust had produced a substantial gun and pointed it at Imre. Imre backed off toward the window, cool as ever. Hugo realized how one could be a knave and yet be brave — it was worth remembering.

"Is that a gun I see, Zoltan? What on earth are you doing?"

"He had no orders, Hugo." Fust was already regaining his famous confidence and verve. "You've ruined everything, you slimy little shit, with your slimy little wrists," he said to Imre by the window. "We were making progress. We were getting people in line. Sure, we gave them things. We even gave them bishops. But we had the country running smoothly." He turned his attention back to Hugo. "Then this bastard came along."

"What do you propose to do?" Imre asked.

"I'm not going back," Fust said. "I've arranged for political asylum."

"You're mad," Imre said. He started to move away from the window.

"Don't move."

"May I sit down?"

"Hugo, give him your chair." Hugo moved the chair near the window. Behind Imre, in the city below, the bulbous dome of a church was glinting in the afternoon sun. Fust motioned Hugo to step back. Imre, after all, did not sit.

"This may be awkward. What to do with His Reverence here and myself?" Imre said.

"I have to go," Hugo interjected. "I'm expected at a meeting. The conclave — remember?"

"Don't move," Fust warned. "Not yet. I need to know your plans." With a wave of the gun he indicated Imre. "If I let him go, he'll ruin you. I'll be safe in America. Probably teaching in some college about the philosophy of Marx or co-op farming. But one way or another, Hugo, he'll ruin you, my boy."

"Not much I can do about that."

"I'll do it for you. I owe it to you, Hugo. A favor from Uncle Georg." Uncle Georg's verve was fully restored.

"Who else knows about me, Zoltan?" Hugo asked.

"No one who cares, Hugo."

"I can't do it."

Fust took off his expensive jacket and threw it over a chair. The gun never wavered. He began to whistle some lively melody that Hugo did not recognize. Hugo felt giddy. If I were Imre, he was thinking, I'd consider this behavior an ominous omen. More than giddy, he felt almost happy. Uncle Georg was back on the job. He might kill everyone, including Hugo, and ruin the Party to which he had given his tacky life, but Fust being in charge again seemed to restore some infernal equilibrium to the world. The devil wasn't dead — he had only been napping. With the gun Fust was indicating the double doors that led to one of the bedrooms.

"All you have to do, Hugo, is go through those doors."

"Don't even think about it," Imre warned.

There were Picasso prints on the wall. One figure had an eye in the back of his head. It too must be a symbol of something, though he could not say what. And anyway there was a woman with an eye near the top of her nose. You could read what you wanted into life. Hugo stood there transfixed. Neither the seminary nor Uncle Georg nor life in any of its manifestations had provided him with a formula for what to do next.

"We've come so far, Hugo," Fust was saying. "He has no right to stop us now."

"Don't go," Imre was practically pleading.

"For what it's worth, Imre," Hugo said, "may the Lord have mercy on your soul."

"Don't go." Imre now feisty again. "I forbid you to go."

Hugo looked Imre steadily in the eye, silently blaming him for all the wrongs of the world, as he backed slowly, deliberately into the bedroom, then pulled the double doors behind him until they clicked closed.

The bedroom was dominated by a magnificent bed. Hugo went to the window, threw it open, gulped in the fresh Italian air. The talk next door was low. It came through as a mumble that Hugo tried not to hear Then there was a dull pop that was quite distinct, followed by a silence. On the bed was Imre's suitcase, and on top of it a little heap of new shirts and underwear in their cellophane wrappings.

Chapter Twenty-Two

"Veni, Creator Spiritus." More than a hundred cardinals came waddling in a crooked line into the Sistine Chapel in what was supposed to be a procession. They sang hoarsely and seldom together, mostly old men, calling down God's unpredictable Spirit to show them how to cast their votes.

The pudgy Cardinal Carfino had his head high and confident. One old cardinal was already sitting down, sickly. At the end of the row was Ladislaus. He had told Hugo of atrocities back home. Three men were gunned down for making a peaceful protest. It mattered to Ladislaus what happened to the church. There were threats to cut government subsidies, which had made the church dependent, as Hugo long ago predicted they would.

"Did they try to tell you how to vote?" Hugo had asked Ladislaus.

"God, no, they wouldn't dare."

An American cardinal was looking in wonder at the ceiling on which Michelangelo — laying for years on his back — painted a masterpiece. There were two rows of seats on either side of the chapel, all facing each other. The cardinals filed into their preordained places, some singing and others gawking around, guided by a team of efficient monsignors.

The Camerlengo, a glorified master of ceremonies appointed by the dead pope to run the church until a successor was elected, now rose to his feet. "My dear brothers," he read from a sheet of green paper, "this conclave is the most solemn act most of us are likely to perform in our lifetimes. Because we are human, we need to be reminded that the only consideration in electing a new pontiff is the will of God and the good of the church...."

Hugo was in the front row. Beside him was an Indian cardinal who looked sideways at him and smiled nervously. There would be two votes in the morning and two in the afternoon, after siesta, the Camerlengo went on. Talk turned to whispering and then to silence. Each man was alone now. All the discussing was over: about who would be a caring pope, or who would be a learned pope, or who would keep the Roman bureaucracy in check from riding roughshod, or who would have the humility, when the curtains were drawn at the end of the day, to kneel down and pray to God for the world.

On every desk was a pencil and several slips of paper, the ballot, which said: "I Elect as Supreme Pontiff." Hugo wrote the word "Nadalet" and folded the paper. He looked around the big room at his colleagues. Some were hesitating, torn no doubt by all the debates, although debating was frowned upon and canvassing forbidden entirely; not to mention the impossibility of knowing the exact will of a God who was notoriously reluctant to come down and tap people on the shoulder, even cardinals.

The Indian already had his pen poised over the second ballot. Ladislaus, on the other side of the aisle, yawned. He probably voted for me, Hugo figured with a pang, just this first token vote; I should have returned the favor — Ladislaus, pope with the pipe.

Four cardinals were collecting the ballots in gold chalices, another ancient tradition. They counted the votes at a table out front, then recounted them. The required majority was two-thirds plus one.

One cardinal received the ballots from another and read them aloud: "...Romberger, Carfino, Carfino, Browne, Carfino, Nadalet, Nadalet, Ovath, Arns, Heckler, Arns, Ovath, Nadalet..."

Outside, in St. Peter's Square, were thousands of people drawn from all corners of the world by the mystique of the papacy and the media hype and the simple belief of those who hold in maximum esteem the man they regard as God's vicar on earth.

"One of the best-known pieces of architecture in Christendom is that little chimney behind me," a television reporter, his back to the basilica, was saying to the camera. "If the smoke comes out black, that means no one has been elected. But if the smoke is white, then we have a new pope."

Nothing was left to chance. They put damp straw into an ugly little stove with the inconclusive ballots, and to be doubly sure they added black chemicals. The Camerlengo held up a lighter before setting the straw on fire. "A technological advance," he said, and the cardinals laughed because they were nervous and needed a laugh.

Between ballots, some went to the bathroom, old men with worn-out bladders. Others talked in a restrained, whispering way.

"The next vote will begin to put a shape on things," Hugo said to the Indian.

"And you got five votes," the Indian said. He smiled a lot. "Who knows what will happen next time!"

"Don't worry," Hugo reassured him lightly. "They won't waste their votes a second time."

"Silence, please." The Camerlengo was again on his feet. "We will now proceed with the second ballot."

Once again Hugo voted for Nadalet. Already the Indian was finished and alert for the next move. Hugo could imagine him running a tight ship in Bombay.

As they called out the names it was clear that the field was narrowing. Carfino got forty-three votes, Nadalet thirty, the German Romberger sixteen. A dozen others were scattered around. Hugo got three. That meant two had abandoned his ship already. There would be no need to run away. Once again the damp straw and ballots were burned.

They broke for lunch. They sat at tables of six or eight. Hugo shared a table with Ladislaus and Pogioli and three others.

"We may be here until Christmas," Ladislaus said.

"Did you notice our friend here, Ovath, getting five votes?" said the always benign Pogioli.

"And did you notice it was down to three on the second vote?" Hugo reminded them.

"Do you think God has anything to do with it?" a cardinal from South America asked.

"Only remotely," Ladislaus answered. "God gives us brains and expects us to use them."

After lunch, some walked in the cramped courtyard while the majority took a siesta, emerging bleary-eyed just before four in the afternoon to catch a breath of fresh air and nose around for rumors and trends.

When the third ballot was counted, the charismatic Romberger had dropped almost out of contention. Positions were hardening. Beronio, a South American, got a surprising ten votes — someone had been busy on his behalf at siesta time. Hugo's count dwindled to two. He hoped the loyal Ladislaus was not wasting a perfectly good vote on him when it ought to be going to Nadalet.

The fourth and last vote of the day was equally inconclusive. The mood at dinner was not so much depression as resignation. Cardinals always hoped for a short conclave, in part to show the world how united they were, but especially because they wanted to go home, unused to rubbing shoulders so intimately with so many other old codgers like themselves. Blue chairs were placed in the corridor so they could wait in comfort for their turn at the bathroom. Many complained about the food, because there was either too much pasta on the menu or not enough. Someone left toothpaste behind on a sink, without the cap, until it fell on the floor where someone else walked on it.

Hugo shared a table with the Indian and seven others from various countries. The Third World men asked him questions about a dozen candidates, and he tried to answer as truthfully as he could while at the same time arguing that Nadalet was the man.

"Beronio may be best in a stalemate," one said.

"Would you please pass the lasagna," said old Aquila from North Africa.

"A stalemate is exactly what we have." Hugo realized that what he enjoyed most about the conclave was the gossip factor: who was rising or falling and why and who were dark horses and why. Carfino and six others were huddled in a corner. Romberger was laughing and happy at a large table — probably, Hugo thought, because his star had faded and now he would never have to carry all those millions of souls on his back.

"We need a reformer," the Indian said.

"We need a saint," another said.

"We need more lasagna," Aquila said.

Out on the square, next morning, the television anchorman was saying to the camera that day two was about to begin and already the experts were guessing there might be a stalemate.

As they shuffled into the Sistine Chapel, Ladislaus poked Hugo with his pipe. "I took your advice and voted for Nadalet," he said. The so-called outside world believed they never broke the rules, for instance by divulging whom they voted for, but the cardinals were after all the ones who made the rules and had long ago decided what was important in life or in conclaves.

"If he doesn't make it this morning, he's finished," Hugo responded. Ladislaus was never stupid enough to give you even a token vote, Hugo dryly said to himself.

"We have plenty of time," Ladislaus said. Hugo could see he'd be sorry when the excitement was over.

The next ballot sounded like a broken record: Carfino, Nadalet, Nadalet, Carfino, Beronio, Carfino...

The Indian sat looking in a mirror. Hugo was perplexed until he realized that the wily friendly fellow was unobtrusively admiring Michelangelo's frescoes on the ceiling.

"Beronio would prefer living in the slums. He would turn down the papacy." Hugo sat with yet a different group of cardinals at lunch.

"Never, Hugo — you can't turn it down."

"Sure, you can."

"As recently as 1922, Cardinal Laurenti turned it down," a cardinal said. "That's how we got Pius XI."

But the Nadalet and Carfino camps were so entrenched that the talk was turning to alternatives. There was wider talk about Beronio. In the first afternoon session the South American got thirty votes. Hugo got thirteen.

"Congratulations," the Indian said.

Out on the square, the crowds watched and then groaned their disappointment as black smoke once again emerged from the little tin chimney.

On the last ballot of the day, Beronio had thirty-two, Hugo thirty-two, Metz twelve.

"It's looking dangerous," the Indian said. From Bombay, Hugo thought dryly, one pope probably looked much like another, so it was easy for this nice man to be content. He and God knew the Indians best and would do the job their own way no matter who was pope.

"It's looking dangerous." Ladislaus repeated the warning as they left the chapel. "Want to go for a walk?"

"What I want is to run away." And it might be a long way to run — Fust had landed him in a royal pickle.

Hugo, standing by the window in Imre's hotel room and hearing the ambiguous pop next door, had been assailed by questions and confusion. The ambiguous pop on another day would be a champagne bottle uncorked for celebration, he and Fust talking dirty about how to fix the world. But on that day — only days earlier — the pop had come from a gun, and at that point, standing by the window, Hugo had not known if Fust or Imre had been shot.

Hugo in one big step had pounced on Imre's suitcase on the bed, the packages of underwear sliding to the floor. Everything was neat inside. And down at the bottom, one of Hugo's books. The book was about how to make a rosy world for everyone at the same time, with no losers, only winners. Could Imre have read it? Everywhere there were surprises. Hugo guessed Imre had not found time to read it.

Also at the bottom of the case, a gun. No surprise — Hugo had counted on it. A relic from the world of winners and losers. Hugo guessed there might be other guns in the room — if you go the gun route you need plenty of them, just in case. But for now one was enough. He checked the bullets in it — six.

At issue was who would come through the door, the crucial ambiguity. He had confidence in Fust. But if wily Imre turned the tables on Uncle Georg, Hugo would need to kill him. He would do it at once, no talk or bargaining, which was how tables often got turned. Theologians might debate whether this procedure was for the good of the church, which held martyrs in high esteem, but Hugo had little trouble putting his conscience at rest.

And Uncle Georg? Hugo had promised himself for years that he would kill Fust the first chance he got. And, indeed, it had been Fust who appeared, closing the double doors behind him. They each stood confronted by the other's gun. Fust first and then Hugo threw the gun on the bed.

"Please forgive me, Hugo, for putting you on the spot like that."

"Is he dead?"

"Try to understand, my boy. Killing you would have caused Imre as much grief as killing, let's say, a fly. Perhaps less — he had a peculiar soft spot for the flora and fauna."

"It's murder," Hugo said.

"Try and see it as self-defense."

"And I'm as guilty as you are — God Almighty!"

"It beats being dead, Hugo. I would have killed you."

"You?" Hugo backed away from him.

"I never got that political asylum."

"You're mad," Hugo said.

"You'll make a good pope, Hugo, I know it."

"Mad," Hugo repeated, beginning to go crazy. "You're fucking mad.

You don't go killing people to get the right pope in place. There are a hundred and ten old men over there and they have the damnedest histories and some of them think the damnedest things. You'd be amazed the way their heads work, never mind that they blame God when their heads . . . Fuck, why am I telling you this? Good God, I could almost have taken that job if they ever offered it, but not now. . . ."

"Please, Hugo." Fust knelt down by the bed. He seemed as if he might cry, talking quietly with an unaccustomed quiver of the lip. "I said a good pope, God damn it, not a good Communist." He brightened, then smiled. "You were never much of a Communist, Hugo. But up there, with those old men, I think you could put something together, patch something up, stop the people from being stupid and put an end to some of the crap and some of the hate. You want to hear something? I'm lost, Hugo. I'll go to hell anyway. Not that there's a hell, because they haven't yet figured out how to make an equitable hell that would do everyone justice. . . ." His head was now down on the bed.

"Is there any chance Imre might be alive?"

"You know what I'm sorry for?" He raised his head again. "Not Imre, I'm sorry for that little bastard of a bishop we shot that day at the old monastery." He got up from his knees and looked Hugo in the eye. "When you become pope, Hugo, would you do me one favor? Canonize that little bishop."

"Bonkers," Hugo said. "Crazy."

"And now, if you'll excuse me, I need to find another hotel." He shook Hugo's hand. "If you don't tell what happened here, neither will I — and the Italians won't want an international incident. Here, this way." He guided Hugo to the elevator, avoiding the deceased Imre in the living room. "We'll meet again," he said in his Uncle Georg manner.

There was a new atmosphere as the electors convened for the third day, a little wave of optimism. When the first count was done, Hugo's name came out of the chalice most frequently. He sat looking down, unable to tell them what a moronic thing they were doing and that the Holy Spirit was deserting them at a crucial moment in the history of the world.

"I'm praying for you," the Indian said, shy now, presuming he was talking to a future pope.

Out on St. Peter's Square, the crowds had grown greater. The television cameras were dividing their attention between the tin chimney above and the people below squinting for a hint of a new pope.

Inside, there was one more vote before lunch. And Hugo could think of no gimmick to stall the cardinals. So he wrote "Ladislaus Bernos" on his ballot and placed it in the chalice. It was all Ladislaus's fault for not having found him out ages ago before he ruined Jeno's life and crapped on the world at large. Up on the ceiling, Michelangelo's God was stretching out a creative finger to spark life into Adam. Fine — but not far away, on another panel, implacable old God was driving the same Adam out of Paradise for hexing the world almost before it had begun.

The votes were collected. One old prelate unfolded them and handed them to another who read them: Ovath, Ovath, Ovath. A small handful holding out for Carfino. One lonely vote for Ladislaus. Soon a growing whisper of excitement rippled through the ranks. The majority of two-thirds plus one was soon reached. A mathematically minded cardinal was keeping score and began clapping at the magic number. Others joined in. Then rose to their feet. Except Hugo. Looking down at the floor and looking solemn. They had him trapped, all doors locked. He looked up at their warm, reassuring faces. For him whose first purpose it was to scuttle them.

The Camerlengo raised his hands for silence. Go on, blurt it out, the voice in Hugo's head said. Tell them they made a mistake. Tell them you're a Communist. No, not that — too incredible, and besides it may no longer be true. Tell them instead you have heart disease or that you're crazy — which is the honest truth, the voice said. Tell them — in a minute it will be too late.

Six prelates surrounded the Camerlengo, and they came forward in solemn formation to where Hugo was now standing. They stopped in front of him, stiff and solemn.

"Hugo Ovath, do you accept your canonical election as Supreme Pontiff?"

Hugo stood holding his little desk with both hands. Moments passed, then became minutes. Cardinals' faces turned from smiling to puzzlement to concern. The silence seemed more immense because of the lusty applause that had gone before.

"Does Your Eminence accept?" the Camerlengo tried again.

"Have courage," Hugo heard the Indian whisper at his side. "We want you to be the best priest in the world," Fust had said. What do I do now, Zoltan? Something went wrong back there, Uncle Georg. Your plan has come home to roost.

Finally Hugo looked around at all their faces, around and back again, then looked directly at the Camerlengo.

"I need time. You have taken me by surprise."

"But you have been chosen." That man's life has been so uncomplicated, Hugo thought — as always he thought more thoughts, including irrelevant ones, in the brief time crises allowed. "It is God's will," the old man said softly to Hugo.

"I'm sorry. I appreciate — but I need time to think."

There was a further pause. The Camerlengo looked around the chapel as if in search of a higher authority, but there was none.

"It is unusual," he said. "We will break for lunch. Then we will return as usual at four." The Camerlengo and his entourage withdrew, their faces solemn, to the sanctuary.

"Benedicamus Domino," he dismissed them.

"Deo gratias," the cardinals answered. In dismay they began to file out. The Indian squeezed Hugo's arm before leaving. "I'm praying for you," he said. Hugo nodded his appreciation. There was so much good in the world, as well as all the crap. Many cardinals looked at him. He knew they were smiling their encouragement, but he did not meet their gaze — there was a chance they might want his hide before sundown.

When everyone had gone he approached the stony faced Camerlengo by the altar.

"I would like to see Ladislaus. After he has finished lunch."

Out in St. Peter's Square, the pilgrims and gawkers had settled down to eating lunch from their brown bags. There was a buzz of excitement. No one was sure what it meant when no smoke, black or white, came from the tin chimney.

Chapter Twenty-Three

In the big sacristy of high ceilings and carved woodwork Hugo paced wall to wall. The Blessed Sacrament was preserved in a gold tabernacle on a small wooden side altar. A red blinking sanctuary lamp hung beside it. It seemed to be saying to Hugo, as he imagined it saying when he was young: I'm on to you.

Ladislaus entered, looking confused. No pipe to brandish now.

"I said you were to finish your lunch."

"I'm fine." Ladislaus already spoke with new deference.

"I want you to hear my confession," Hugo said, looking into the distance through a window.

"Now?"

"Yes, now."

Ladislaus patted his pockets under his robes until he found a little purse from which he took a purple stole, which he draped around his neck. He placed two chairs side by side. "Sit down, then."

"I'd rather kneel." Hugo drew up a kneeler beside Ladislaus. He knelt. He bowed his head for a long moment of silence. "It's forty-one years, at least, since my last good confession." He could not see Ladislaus's face above him, expressionless as a rock. God knew what his sordid story was, but he still had to put it into words for the sacrament. It was a rule of the game: to take nothing away, cut no corners.

"Go on."

"The only reason I became a priest was to infiltrate the church for the Communists. I did not believe any of it. Year in, year out, I pretended. I betrayed people and sent some to their deaths."

Hugo's eyes were closed. Ladislaus was looking ahead into space.

"I was the one who reported on Jeno." He paused for a long time — if necessary, giving Ladislaus time to strike him dead. Or at least walk out on him. "I had an illicit relationship with a woman. I did everything you can imagine with her, short of the full sexual act. I offered sacrilegious Masses, every one of them without exception." He stopped.

"When did you stop believing?"

"I don't remember. I joined the Party when I was eighteen." Long pause.

"I used to see you praying."

"I was pretending." Hugo wanted to tell about the times he tried not to pretend. It might soften Ladislaus to know that he at times took running leaps at faith; that at times he asked for things as if he believed, such as heaven for his mother, after he had asked for her recovery and failed to get it. But he said none of this to Ladislaus.

"Is that it all?"

"There is one other thing. Murder. Just the other day. I helped one Communist kill another. Do you remember Uncle Georg?"

"Was he the killer?"

"It's very complicated."

"Are you sorry?"

"Of course I'm sorry. But I can't say I wouldn't do it again — as I say, it's complicated."

"What else?"

"That's most of it. The big stuff. I was caught in the end without time to prepare."

"God stole up on you."

"I can't see any God, Ladislaus. I can't hear him or touch him or come to grips with him."

"If you could see him," Ladislaus said, suddenly gripped by a fierce anger as the immensity of the story sank in. He spat out the words above Hugo's still bowed head: "If you could come to grips, as you say, God damn it, he wouldn't be God — you lying, deceiving son of a bitch. . . ." He stopped to compose himself, an old man breathing heavily. What if he gets a heart attack, Hugo's inner voice prompted. As if you were not in enough hot water already. "Why did you decide to confess?" Ladislaus asked.

"I have no idea. It's ironic, isn't it? We all get jostled around by life, but I got a bigger jostle than most. The church rubbed off on me, and here I am. But the Party too rubbed off on me, and Imre is dead. If you want to know what I really think — I think I was hoping you'd expose me. Or kill me. That somehow you'd solve it for me, Ladislaus."

"I'll give you absolution," Ladislaus said after another long pause. "You'll have to decide whether it's worth anything. Make the act of contrition."

While Hugo mumbled the act of contrition, Ladislaus took the precaution of giving him only conditional absolution, punctuated by a tight little sign of the cross: "In quantum capax es, ego te absolvo a peccatis tuis, in nomine Patris et Filii et Spiritus Sancti, Amen."

Ladislaus wasted no time standing up, pulling the little stole from around his neck and flinging it on the floor. With fierce energy he kicked the chair on which he had been sitting so that it slid on the sleek marble floor to the opposite wall where it stopped with a thud. He strode toward the door as if eager to escape. Then he turned around. His words were squeezed out through suppressed anger: "You could do great work for the Party here. And with the seal of confession I won't be able to tell."

He turned to leave. Hugo got to his feet. He looked broken. He sounded almost inaudible.

"Don't go yet." Ladislaus turned around but stayed by the door. "You have to tell me what to do," Hugo's voice was begging.

The anger began welling up again in Ladislaus, and he paced back and forth.

"Take out the damn pipe and light it," Hugo encouraged. "I'm the nearest thing they have to a pope. I can give you permission." But Ladislaus ignored him. Back and forth. Then he threw himself against the little wooden altar, hammering it with his fists. He bounced his head against it, sobbing uncontrollably. Still sobbing, he turned on Hugo.

"I must have looked so stupid, Hugo, when I was swallowing all those lies. And promoting you. And telling you secrets — tell me honestly, did I look stupid?"

"No, Ladislaus, never..."

"And did you despise us all? And what in God's name were you thinking when you shit on us like that? If I was man enough I'd kill you just for Jeno, for poor Jeno, and for us all, for all the lies, and..."

"I always loved you, Ladislaus."

"God damn you, Hugo, may you rot in hell."

"I love you, Ladislaus." Hugo was now crying too, great big sobs.

"And I'd rot in hell to bring Jeno back; I swear I would; I'd happily rot in hell for Jeno. Help me, Ladislaus, help me."

Hugo moved forward sobbing and threw himself into the arms of Ladislaus, and they embraced at length, both sobbing, their words an incantation. "God damn you, God damn you, God damn you," Ladislaus was saying. "Help me Ladislaus, help me, help me," Hugo was saying.

They pulled apart and composed themselves with the help of big white handkerchiefs pulled from under their soutanes. Ladislaus moved up again to the little wooden altar. He knocked on the tabernacle door as Jeno had once done for a joke when they were young and learning to say Mass.

"The heart of our story, Hugo, is a forgiving God. Infinitely forgiving. If he can't forgive you, he can't forgive anyone. You could be one of the great test cases, a renegade like you."

"I can't, Ladislaus. Look at me — I can't."

"Jesus forgave everyone he could get his hands on. He could turn you into one of the great popes, because you would be coming to the world in humility — and by God you have plenty to be humble about."

"Often, Ladislaus, I came very close to believing. It was a fearful thing. There were those moments when — when I could almost touch something, and it might have been God. . . ."

"Go on, go on," Ladislaus encouraged him desperately. He had taken the pipe out of his pocket but diligently refrained from lighting it. "When the moment is right there's nothing to it. It's as easy as taking a blind leap off a cliff into the ocean. . . ."

"One other thing, Ladislaus. One day you told me that the missing bishop, little Bishop Illyes, had a drinking problem, and that without the support of the booze he might have reneged and made some kind of confession. I want you to know that it's not true."

"How do you know?" Ladislaus was wide-eyed.

"He embraced one of the men who was designated to shoot him, and then he stood there, calm as you — hell, calmer than you — and looked up at the sky full of contentment." Hugo began to weep again, standing in the middle of the floor until Ladislaus put a chair under him. "They shot him, Ladislaus. He stood there looking peaceful and — and brave. I swear this is true. Tell everyone, will you?"

Ladislaus stared in amazement at Hugo. Then he looked about the sacristy for inspiration or some clue. There was none. It was a day to look inward and not outside for clues. He looked at his watch.

"What will you do?"

"Pick a good one, Ladislaus." Hugo rose from the chair and put it away by the wall. "One who can leap off that cliff every day. And take everyone with him."

"But not you?"

"Not me. Go back now to your lunch, and take a little nap. There's a lot of work ahead, and you're not as young as you used to be."

They embraced. Then stood back looking at each other, collecting what might be last impressions. When Ladislaus turned he did not look back, an old man walking slowly through the sacristy door.

The sky was Roman blue. The noise of crazy traffic threatened to bring down the city. Tourists emerged from old streets with maps and cameras, darting between motorcycles. Closer to the Trevi Fountain, the cascading waters soothed the weary pilgrim. Fust was sitting on the wall where, just days earlier, Hugo sat and waited. His umbrella and briefcase were resting on his knee. He was wearing a jaunty white jacket, and his cocky hat and his restless eyes were busy taking in the crowd of tourists taking photos and throwing coins and smooching for the cameras and for fun.

Eventually Fust could see, in the distance, limping along with the help of a cane, Hugo. He was dressed in a black suit but without roman collar, a blood-red shirt open at the neck, and a bruised, weather-beaten version of the wide-brimmed Roman hat that he had earlier begged Ladislaus to discard. The ensemble, Fust thought, looked shabby. Then he thought it might be the man and not the clothes who was under the weather. He was moving slowly, needing the cane. He also needed a shave.

At a certain distance Hugo stopped to observe. Fust watched him carefully but made no move. Then Hugo spotted Fust, and stopped again, start and stop, several times, until he was only a few feet away.

"Sit down, you look tired," Fust said.

"Are you going to shoot me, Zoltan?"

"What the hell is going on?"

"I'm serious. If you have orders to shoot me, all I ask is that you not delay it." He moved closer. "I'd welcome it, Zoltan." A trace of bravado then came to the surface. "Hell, I even made my confession."

"Here, sit down," Fust encouraged. After a hesitation Hugo sat beside him on the low wall. "I'm not going back, Hugo."

"They elected me, Zoltan."

"I'll ask for asylum. I'll start all over. I'll think of something."

"God damn it, Zoltan, did you hear what I said? I could have been pope."

Fust heard him at last. He stood up, faced Hugo, came closer. "Really?"

"It was a great plan, Zoltan. It's just that — I don't know, something went wrong back there...."

"Pope, huh?"

They stood in the beautiful sun looking at each other, trying to figure out what happened back there, trying to adjust to the new reality, whatever it might be. Hugo, inspired, flagged down a tourist with his cane.

"Would you, as a favor, take a photo of my friend and me?" The tourist smiled, lined them up, snapped the picture, while the two stood haughtily looking into the romantic fountain. The quizzical tourist asked what she ought to do with the picture.

"Send it to Hugo, in care of the Vatican. They'll know what to do." The tourist nodded and smiled and waved and seemed surprised that a tramp like Hugo should speak a foreign language.

An hour later, Fust and Hugo stopped to buy American hamburgers from a vendor outside the bulky, brooding Castel Sant' Angelo.

"Let me pay," Fust said. "I have lashings of money. And everyone knows that people like you are poor."

"The best priest in the world, you said. I gave them a run for their money, didn't I?" He attacked the hamburger with enthusiasm.

The excitement was growing as Hugo and Fust trudged through the growing crowd of pilgrims in St. Peter's Square. The two men squinted and climbed until they could see the tin chimney. Each was drinking a coke.

"Are we too old, Hugo, to start over?" Fust was his old self again. "Maybe a new order, or a crusade or something? So long as there's no fasting involved — I hate hunger."

He was interrupted by a woman. "There's smoke!" she shouted. A momentary hush fell on the square as everyone strained to look.

"It's black," Fust said.

The color of the smoke, as frequently happens, was at first indeterminate, the straw and the ballots trying to get their act together.

"No, no, that's not black smoke," Hugo shouted. People turned to look at him. "It's white, I tell you."

"We have a pope!" The people went wild with that strange delight reserved for new popes bringing fresh visions of hope or some damn thing to keep the world going round.

OTHER CROSSROAD NOVELS YOU MIGHT ENJOY

Joan Ohanneson

SCARLET MUSIC

Hildegard of Bingen: A Novel

"Ohanneson has dramatized the life of twelfth-century
Hildegard of Bingen in this fascinating novel.
Highly recommended."

— *Library Journal*

"Like an episode of Masterpiece Theater
at its most arresting and enlightening."

— Eugene Kennedy

0-8245-1646-X; $14.95

Asta Scheib

CHILDREN OF DISOBEDIENCE

The Love Story of Martin Luther and Katharina of Bora

A sweeping historical novel that traces the unconventional friendship
of two unusual and unforgettable people. The marriage of Martin Luther
to the nun Katherine of Bora took place in a period that rocked
the church and the world. Well researched and poetically written,
this novel gives a sensitive account of their relationship and a
vivid sense of the tumultuous time in which they lived.

0-8245-1695-8; $14.95

Please support your local bookstore, or call 1-800-395-0690.
For a free catalog, please write us at
THE CROSSROAD PUBLISHING COMPANY
370 LEXINGTON AVENUE, NEW YORK, NY 10017

We hope you enjoyed The Nolan. *Thank you for reading it.*

crossroad